Joan Moules lived in London from 1940 to 1945 before returning to Hastings. From working in various offices she was plunged into the life of a busy shopkeeper when she married. Joan lives by the sea in Selsey, Sussex. She has two daughters, five grandchildren and two cats. She writes fiction and non-fiction, and among her many other interests are reading, walking, the theatre, music hall and Victorian jewellery.

SCRIPT FOR MURDER

It's 1955. In the seaside town of Fairbourne, on the south coast of England, is the Victoriana theatre. One of the actors has been murdered in his dressing room at a time between the matinée and the evening performance. Everyone working in the theatre falls under suspicion, especially the cast and the murdered man's wife, who is more famous than her husband. Inspector Carding and Sergeant George Binns investigate, whilst the actors, used to playing a part, suspect one another. Yet to leave before the season finishes will point the finger at the murderer . . .

JOAN M. MOULES

SCRIPT FOR MURDER

Complete and Unabridged

ULVERSCROFT
Leicester

First published in Great Britain in 2009 by
Robert Hale Limited.
London

First Large Print Edition
published 2010
by arrangement with
Robert Hale Limited.
London

The moral right of the author has been asserted

British Library CIP Data

Moules, Joan.
   Script for murder.
   1. Actors- -Death- -Fiction. 2. Theaters- -Fiction.
   3. Murder- -Investigation- -Fiction. 4. Detective and
   mystery stories. 5. Large type books.
   I. Title
   823.9′14–dc22

ISBN 978-1-44480-064-7

Published by
F. A. Thorpe (Publishing)
Anstey, Leicestershire

Set by Words & Graphics Ltd.
Anstey, Leicestershire
Printed and bound in Great Britain by
T. J. International Ltd., Padstow, Cornwall

This book is printed on acid-free paper

For Peter and Jax
With love and my thanks for all your help
and encouragement

1

SPRING 1955

Betty Morse boarded the train bound for Fairbourne at Victoria railway station. She had said goodbye to her mother and Lillee at home as she always did. It was easier that way. She settled herself into an empty seat by the window and closed her eyes. She knew from past experience that the images would fade as the train moved nearer to its destination, but for that first half of the journey they were so close to the top it felt as though her body was breaking into tiny pieces.

To distract herself she thought about next week. She wasn't looking forward to it. Murder wasn't her usual objective — for her this was a first time and she was worried in case she made a hash of it. For a start she wasn't used to guns, but then practice makes perfect, she thought, and on the night she would be concentrating so hard there surely wouldn't be time to feel fear.

The whistle blew and they were off, rumbling out of Victoria station, the rhythm of the wheels echoing the words in her head. *Kill him, kill him, kill him*, they seemed to be shouting at her, drumming it into her like the beat of jungle tom-toms.

Briefly she opened her eyes as the train crossed the River Thames and she wondered how long it would be before she was back with her mother and daughter for a day's visit. It would have been lovely if she could have had Lillee with her. Apart from her own longing for her daughter, the sea air would be better for her than the smog in London. But it gave her peace of mind to know her child was loved and cared for so much when she had to be away. For a few moments her mind went back to Lillee's fourth birthday party two weeks ago. She replayed the afternoon in her mind — the little girl's bright eyes and enchanting smile when they lit the candles on her cake and her enormous puff as she tried to blow out all four together.

Clouds of smoke from the engine billowed past the window and Betty closed her eyes again and concentrated on what she was going to say and do next week. *I've had enough. You have a choice. Give her up completely or I pull the trigger. Either way she will never see you again.* She hoped her hand wouldn't tremble as she pointed the gun at him. Poison would have been a better method because she wouldn't need a steady hand for that; he would be the one to pick up the glass and drink the contents.

This hand tremble had only come on her a couple of weeks ago but already it had resulted in two broken cups and a plate. She put it down to nerves and stress, which manifested itself in all sorts of ways. Last time it had been migraines and the one before she had lost her voice for two days. Every time she opened her mouth, only a flimsy whisper escaped. It was fine again once she was there, of course, but terrifying beforehand.

The train was slowing down; must be coming into East Croydon. One person alighted and a crowd of noisy youngsters came into the carriage. They looked round then went into the corridor and moved along, still chatting nineteen to the dozen. An elderly woman sat down in the seat facing her and, after smiling at her briefly, Betty resolutely closed her eyes again. She didn't want to hear someone's life story just now, and so often complete strangers did just that, told her all about themselves and their problems. Her mother said it was because she had a sympathetic face, but she didn't believe that. She thought it was simply someone for them to talk to. Well, just this once she didn't want to listen to anyone else's troubles; she had enough of her own. Clutching her handbag tightly, she rehearsed in her mind yet again the words she would say to Adam when she confronted him with the gun in her hand. A non-trembling hand, she fervently hoped, because it would be such a farce if she missed.

She dozed uncomfortably, strangely aware of being in two worlds at the same time. In one she was about to kill Adam and in the other she was still on the train venturing into the unknown.

As they approached the next station, the rowdy group of teenagers made their way back along the corridor and past the open compartment door. They were whooping and shouting as they discussed the previous day's football matches.

''*Shoot man, shoot,' we were yelling, but he still missed a bloody obvious goal.'*

The excited voice startled Betty from her nap. The word 'shoot' burnt itself into her brain and she leapt to her feet. 'I've killed him, oh my God, I've shot the man I love dead.'

The woman sitting in the opposite seat stood up too. 'Are you all right, dear?' she said. 'Is something wrong?'

Betty, still more in the dream where she was pointing the gun at Adam than in the train travelling to Fairbourne, felt in her pocket for a handkerchief. The lady, who was the only other occupant of the carriage, misread her action, grabbed her own bag from the seat and dashed off into the corridor.

Wide awake now, Betty hurried to the gap and looked up and down but there was no sign of the obviously frightened woman. As long as she doesn't report a madwoman on the train, she thought. A slow smile emerged as she saw the funny side of the situation, and fully realized that she had spoken out loud. How could that poor lady know that while she was asleep she was running through the lines of the play she was in next week? It was her favourite tried and tested method, letting her unconscious mind absorb and remember. It usually worked and she seldom had problems with learning the script of a new play. She had never spoken her lines out loud in public when rehearsing before, though. Her dilemma this time was the play's content, for it was a murder and so far in her career she had played only romantic parts. She was worried that her voice was too light and didn't carry the conviction that would be needed for the role of revengeful murderess.

The whistle blew and the train moved slowly out of the station, and for the next half hour Betty was on tenterhooks every time someone walked through the corridor in case they were coming to see if she had a gun in her pocket. No-one did and she assumed the woman had thought she was having a bad dream.

Panic set in as she walked down the steps at Fairbourne railway station but the police were not waiting there either. Simply the ticket collector. Betty gave him a beaming smile as she went through with her suitcase.

★ ★ ★

Fairbourne was a reasonably sized seaside resort. It had a good promenade, at least two miles long, a sandy beach when the tide was out and, being on the south coast, a warm climate. There was a floral clock on the seafront near the pier, which spelt out WELCOME in small flowers of different colours. This was surrounded by low white-painted railings to stop children trampling across it or trying to pick the flowers. It was more of a warning fence than anything else because even a very small child could have climbed over had they been determined or unsupervized.

The town had a good variety of shops, spread out among the five streets which emanated from the clock tower. Liptons and Home & Colonial were on the same one, but Sainsbury's, which was larger, was in the busiest one near to Woolworths.

The part of the town she liked best, however, was to the east. This was the fishermen's quarters and she loved going down there dressed in slacks and T-shirt and wandering among the boats and fish stalls on the beach. The first time she played Fairbourne she discovered this maze of narrow streets and alleys — 'twittens' was the Sussex name for them, one of the fishermen told her. The tightly packed houses and cottages were all so different too. Most of them were old but here and there a newer one had been fitted in, its shape obviously designed to the small area it could occupy. These had been built before the war, but were in keeping with the others, flint and brick, and she could tell that in a few more years when they had weathered even more there would not be much difference in their outward appearance at least.

The house she liked, although she had only seen it from the outside, was tall and thin, its chimney slender and graceful as it rose into the sky. She imagined sitting by the window in the top room and gazing over the rooftops and out to sea.

Betty had a dream that one day she would come here to Fairbourne with Lillee to live. Maybe even get her mum down too; the air here would be good for her weak chest. Sea, countryside within a mile of the town, and only a little over two hours to London. Her ambition to play in the West End one day still smouldered gently inside her. Not the flame it had once been, but still glowing softly. It would be so good to have a place here to come home to after a strenuous tour, but on the money she earned she knew that was a long way off. If she could master the major role in one of the two murder plays this season then who knew what might happen in the future? 'It's a challenge,' she told herself, 'and I'll give it my best shot.'

Half an hour after arriving in Fairbourne she was unpacked and settled into her digs for the coming months and looking forward to her first glimpse of the sea this year. That always calmed her nerves. She recalled an old actress who had once told her that if she didn't suffer a bit beforehand she wouldn't give a good performance. A mild fluttering was one thing, she thought, but this time she was truly worried. Still, the second play they were doing was a romantic comedy and she felt at home with that. If she could get through the first murder without mishap she knew she would feel confident again. Anything new had always thrown her, ever since she was a child. She changed and went out, heading towards the seafront.

She was leaning on the rails near the pier when someone came up close to her.

'Hello. It's Betty, isn't it?'

'Roger! Roger Johnson.' She turned and smiled at him. 'Are you at the Victoriana too?'

'I am. It's good to see a face you know.'

Especially this face, she thought, smiling at him. They had gone out together a few times when they were working up north at the end of last year.

They chatted for a while, and then walked along the seafront together. On the way they passed the Plaza cinema and stopped to see what was showing.

'*The Student Prince*,' Betty said. 'It's had wonderful reviews. Edmund Purdom plays the lead but it's Mario Lanza's voice they use. Must be difficult to do that, I should think.'

Roger looked at the stills outside. 'I expect Purdom sings it to get the right mouth positions and facial expressions and they simply erase his voice and substitute Mario Lanza's. Shall we go and see later on?'

'That sounds like a good idea.' They made a date for the evening. 'I'll meet you here at 6.30,' Roger said. 'That gives us time to settle in and sort ourselves out. Where are you staying?'

'Same digs as last year — I was here then. It's clean and reasonable and only a quarter of an hour's walk from the theatre.'

'I was in Brighton last year for the summer season,' he said, 'and Yarmouth the year before, so haven't first-hand experience of the current lot here, but it looks all right.'

★ ★ ★

Roger was waiting when she arrived at the cinema that evening. They had to queue for some time but it gave them a chance to catch up with their news, and by the time they were ushered into their seats, the programme was in the middle of the feature film, and it seemed to Betty as though they were carrying on their friendship from last year. It could be a good few months. She had been disappointed not to hear from Roger after that last tour, especially as they exchanged addresses. She had not contacted him because of Lillee — it didn't do to tell boyfriends about her beautiful daughter at first — but who knew what this season might bring?

2

The players for the summer season in Fairbourne congregated in the Victoriana theatre at 9.30 on the Monday morning. There were six of them, three men and three women. They were doing four plays over a period of four weeks before starting again with play number one. They changed the programme on Thursdays so that visitors who were on holiday for a fortnight had a chance to see two plays during the two weeks they were in the town. This system had worked well in previous summers, giving them good houses for each performance.

The company who had been in residence in Fairbourne last year were in Eastbourne this time and director Tim Merry had advertised in the stage papers for actors and actresses for the season here. He had auditioned those who applied and chosen his team, but three weeks ago the chap who was to play the lead in most of the plays had died suddenly. He had been injured in a train crash in January when the York to Bristol Express derailed at Sutton Coldfield but had seemed to be fully recovered and had actually spoken to Tim only two days before his unexpected death.

It was a bitter blow for Tim so late in the day, when most likely candidates would already be booked into something else. Then he thought about Arnold Brand, who lived locally. That was when his luck changed, for although Arnold swaggered and preened, telling him he had decided to go abroad later and wasn't sure if he wanted to be part of what he described as 'this little small-town group', he did agree that as he hadn't anything big in the offing he would join the company 'just for this season'.

Tim didn't care much for the actor. 'Too bumptious by half,' he said to his wife, 'but needs must when the devil drives and there is no-one else.'

Once engaged, the cast had been sent scripts and Tim hoped they were all word perfect. There were only three days for rehearsals before the matinee opening on Wednesday and he needed to concentrate on all the other things there were to do when they finally came together.

He had told Len, whom he had worked with for years, that he wouldn't need him until Tuesday to sort out the lights, and the props for each play were stored in the shed immediately behind the Victoriana. It was old but the roof was good, and like the theatre itself it had escaped the bomb that fell further along the seafront on one of the hotels during the war.

Tim was there well before anyone else, arriving from his home a few miles along the coast. He stood outside the theatre, taking in its rather shabby appearance in comparison to the promenade opposite where the council had this year painted the railings a seaside blue. Even the bandstand on the apron of the pier, a little further on, had been spruced up and its polished veneer glinted like mahogany when the sun caught it.

Of course they had to do something to attract the visitors, he thought. In 1947 they had replaced the central part of the pier, which had been removed during the war in case of invasion, and spruced up the rest of the promenade, concentrating mostly on strings of coloured lights and lamppost decorations. But this year the council had actually focused on the frontline itself. The poor old Victoriana, however, was on its own — no-one had the money to give it an overhaul, and because it wasn't bombed during the war it didn't qualify for the war-damage grant which would have helped. Inside needed some renovation too. Some of the cherubs could do with a clean and the carpets certainly showed signs of the many feet that had tramped over them on the way to the plush royal blue seats. Yet it had such wonderful acoustics, Tim thought, and a brilliant line of sight, being modelled on the Frank Matcham theatres of the late eighties and early 1900s. Indeed, it had been built when Fairbourne had first blossomed as a popular watering place and prominent London doctors recommended the seaside to their wealthy patients. It was ideal for any sort of entertainment, from plays through to the music halls it was originally built for.

Arnold Brand lived in Fairbourne although he was often away touring. He walked along to the theatre on that Monday morning wondering how it would be to spend the summer here at home. Especially as his actress wife Iris was going to be there too for most of the time, it seemed. She was starring in the summer show at Eastbourne, having accepted the role while she worked on her one-woman show planned for the West End in the autumn.

They were seldom home together for more than a couple of weeks at a time. He had tired of her within months of the marriage, when he realized that she would not further his career. Hers had taken off like a rocket but none of the glittering fallout from it landed on him. He couldn't believe how wild some of the audiences were about her and how tough she was in keeping his name out of the limelight in connection with her own.

'Iris Brand sounds better than Iris Masters. Would look better in lights too,' he had said to her many times, but she wouldn't budge. 'Masters suits me well enough. I don't need your name to publicize my career, Arnold, and you certainly are not going to use mine to help you get jobs.' There was nothing he could do about it and so he took the opposite view and often denied he was married to the famous Iris Masters; this gave him the freedom to do as he pleased where other women were concerned. Although he wasn't above using her name to young ambitious star-crazed actresses to help his own cause with them.

He knew he hadn't been first choice here and he resented the fact, especially as he had a great deal of experience and, as he put it to himself, 'am taking on leading parts which none of the other men in the company could cope with'. He ignored the facts which Tim Merry, the producer and director, had told him about the man who had died so suddenly. Of course, it made sense not to try to juggle parts around at this late stage and it would give him an edge with them all if he handled it right.

The rest of the cast consisted of Betty Morse, Nicola Coates, Roger Johnson, Prince Kingly and Crystal Holman.

'Good morning, everyone,' Tim said, when they were all assembled on the stage. 'The first play of the season is called *The Swapping Party*. Places, please, and we'll give it a run-through.'

The play opened with three married couples at a supper party, discussing the idea of swapping partners for sex. In the script they were paired off as Arnold and Betty, Nicola and Roger and Crystal and Prince.

'Right, from the top then.'

Betty had the opening line. 'I'm really not sure about this, and I'd like more time to think. I mean, it's not — '

'Oh, for heaven's sake, woman, a change is as good as a rest, they say, and let's face it, our sex life has been rather dull lately.' This from her husband, Adam, played by Arnold.

Betty looked suitably crushed and bit her lip as the rest of them gazed at her with pity and astonishment showing in their faces.

'A lot of people are having swapping parties these days,' Roger chimed in. 'It's the latest craze and it could be fun.'

'Yes, familiarity can breed contempt,' Prince said. 'I'm all for change. Better to do it

16

with each other's consent too, rather than deceitfully.'

Crystal giggled and, looking at Betty, said her first line. '*Our* sex life is anything but dull.' She looked directly at Prince Kingly, her husband in the play, and he gave the thumbs-up sign. 'I don't mind sharing him among friends, though. Be an adventure for us all. More exciting than playing cards.' She giggled again.

'A bit of variety will spice everything up.' Nicola threw her opinion into the pool and it earned her a venomous look from her husband, played by Roger Johnson.

The first ten minutes went well, then Arnold fluffed his lines and improvized.

'Stick to the script,' Tim said quietly.

A prompt came from the wings, where the understudy for all the men's roles, Peter Strong, stood. Arnold muttered something under his breath, which they all ignored, and the rehearsal continued. Five minutes later Arnold did it again. After a couple of seconds, when they all looked towards him, he said the wrong line and, without pausing, elaborated on it. Nicola, who should have been next to speak, looked towards the prompt corner and then stumbled in rather too quickly as the words came through.

Tim drew in a sharp breath but let them

continue. Less than half an hour into the rehearsal Nicola went into a line which came much further into the play and asked if she could use the script just for today.

'For Christ's sake, we open on Wednesday,' Tim said. 'No script. You've had it long enough to be word perfect by now.' Turning to Arnold, who once again had been the cause of it, he said, 'Study your lines and get them right. It isn't fair to anyone if you don't give the correct cue.'

Arnold clenched his fist and banged it heavily on the table. 'I've not had the script that long,' he said, 'and any thespian worth their salt could pick it up from what I said. It's surely better than drying up?'

Betty felt her heart pounding inside her. What a start, and they hadn't even got to the bit she was dreading yet. She glanced down at her hands, which were quite still. She reached for the salt on the table. She wanted to test whether they would stay that way when she picked something up but before she could check it out Tim walked over and said, 'No, Betty, don't distract from the conversation like that. You can wring your hands together if you like but nothing more than that and a worried look. You're the one that's least keen on the idea, remember, and I'm sure you can convey it without too much movement.'

'Personally I think that would be good,' Arnold said. 'She could pick up the salt cellar and twist it round in her hands, then drop it and when it spills we could all tell her to throw some over her left shoulder and — '

'Yes, and it hits someone right in the eye and — ' Prince joined in and Tim said loudly, 'No extra business. This is not a pantomime, it's a serious murder play. Now let's get on with it.'

When both Nicola and Arnold had to be prompted again within five minutes of each other and Roger sat silently when he was asked a question because he said he hadn't heard it and to please face him when they were talking to him, Tim called a break. When they went back to work after even that short space of socializing, the atmosphere was a little easier.

Betty didn't get to test whether her hand would be steady to hold the gun because when it came to that part in the last scene they had no props there and she simply had to imagine it in her hand and aim accordingly. It took about one second.

Tim concentrated on stage directions, positions and nuances but it was not a happy or easy morning and when they finished just before two o'clock he went home with a thumping headache.

The next rehearsal was Tuesday morning, where they would check lighting and sound as well as run through the more stressful parts of the play, and in the afternoon there would be a dress rehearsal with press there for a photo call. If they hadn't got it together properly by then there would need to be yet another run-through on Wednesday morning, Tim thought. He didn't tell the cast this because that tiny spark of optimism that it would work out without more confrontation than was absolutely necessary was still flickering somewhere at the back of his mind.

Through the mists of pain now vibrating inside his head, Tim hoped it would run better than this first day. He couldn't afford to be out of a job and this one was at least close to home. He could sleep in his own bed each night.

3

At first the audiences at the Victoriana were sparse, and although the company worked their socks off the applause was average and they only took one quick curtain call before 'God Save The Queen.'

It was three weeks into the run before things started to improve. There were more visitors about in the town by then. Betty had coped well in that first play with the handling of the gun when she had to shoot her husband Adam, who at that point in the drama was about to leave her for one of the others in the wife-swapping group. Her hand was steady and she realized that by the end of the week her voice was more resonant and realistic for the part. The second play was a comedy, and now they were into their third offering, another murder. Betty was not the killer in this one.

They were getting more people into the theatre and this gave them all a boost and a better bonding with each other, at least during working hours. Even Tim began to relax and only went home with a headache a couple of times a week, usually during the changeover of plays.

'For crying out loud!' he shouted at both Arnold and Nicola when each had gone into a line from the previous play at the Wednesday matinee. The blue velvet curtain had barely swished closed and the cast's hands hadn't dropped from the 'we're all good pals together' bonhomie position.

'Bloody perfectionist,' Arnold said. 'I'd like to see you out here rehearsing next week's play in the morning and doing the current one in the afternoon and evening. You couldn't do it, you cringing, cowering bully. You'd have a bloody nervous breakdown, you would, yet you stand there with the script in your hand and lord it over the ones who are bringing in the money. Don't you forget it's me and the rest of the cast that puts your wage packet in your pocket every week. I could do your job any time, I could, but you couldn't do mine, not in a million years you couldn't.' He stamped across the stage and disappeared into the wings. Nicola looked close to tears and, murmuring 'sorry' as she passed Tim, went through to her dressing room.

When Tim reached home, his wife greeted him with a kiss. 'Don't look so worried, dear, it may never happen,' she said, smiling and gently placing her hand on his hot head.

'It already has. Two of them got their plays mixed up this afternoon.'

She kissed him gently then went off to the kitchen. 'I'll make us a nice cup of tea,' she said. 'And, you know, Tim — ' Her neat figure appeared again in the doorway ' — I don't suppose any of the audience noticed because I daresay all the cast carried on as if nothing was wrong.'

He said softly, 'You are a darling and probably right but *I* noticed. That blasted Arnold it was, and young Nicola followed the cue. He recovered it smoothly enough because it was during a small talk around the table scene and it was easy with his experience to link into the proper line, but it threw her. I lost my temper with them both afterwards,' he added to her retreating back, 'and it ended with a shouting match between that bumptious man and me with Nicola on the verge of tears.'

When she took the tea into him, Tim was sitting in an armchair, his head down and cradled in his hands. She slipped upstairs to the bathroom and got him a couple of Aspros.

'Here, these will ease it, Tim,' she said, 'then maybe you could have a nap before going back this evening. You really must try not to worry so much.'

Meanwhile, back in her dressing room Nicola fought back the tears. She didn't like

Arnold much but he was right about Tim being a bully. Or was he? After all, they should get their lines and plays right; it was part of their job. She wanted to succeed as an actress, but at moments like this she had many doubts as to whether she had chosen the right profession after all. She didn't think she would ever make the big time and she wondered now if she enjoyed the life enough to carry on if she did not get to the top. Maybe she should have stayed with the circus, where she was at least a big fish in a small pool.

Betty came in and said quietly, 'Arnold's asking for trouble, shouting and swearing at Tim like that, I reckon, don't you? He's not exactly star material and Peter would probably make just as good a job of the part. Understudies usually do. Probably without hogging the limelight as Arnold does, and Tim knows that. One day Arnold will push him too far.'

'Mmm,' was all Nicola trusted herself to say. She made for the door then, half turning, said to her roommate, 'Just going to get some fresh air before the evening show, Betty.'

When Nicola had left, Betty sat down in the old basket chair in front of the mirror. She felt sorry for Nicola at the moment, but really the girl had no spunk, no fire. She was

24

like an ornament, beautiful but not especially useful. And she had been paying far too much attention to Roger lately. Betty felt a stab of jealous anger as she recalled Nicola's coy excitement and flushed cheeks when she asked her what she had done on the one day off a week they had. She herself had gone to London to see her mother and Lillee but felt certain that Nicola's date last Sunday had been with Roger, even though she hadn't named him.

Arnold was a disruptive influence in more ways than one — a really nasty man, she thought — and Nicola seemed to be easily upset. She would have to get used to the ups and downs of a theatrical life if she was hoping to get anywhere. That innocent-little-girl look and voice wouldn't help her when she came up against people like Arnold. Betty rose from the chair, wondering where Nicola had gone. Was nice gentle Roger consoling her somewhere? A long sigh escaped unbidden from her lips.

Roger had also been along to Crystal's room several times lately if she could believe the stories on the grapevine. Betty was surprised if he was seeing a married woman because it didn't tie in with her knowledge of him, but then she admitted to herself that she didn't know him well. Not nearly as well as

25

she would have liked.

She was attracted to him and they had worked well together before. Even so, it was almost the end of the tour last year when he had asked her out and nothing more had come of it.

The next afternoon they bumped into each other by the fishermen's net shops in the old town, the name by which the fishing quarter was generally known.

'One of my favourite spots here,' she said as they ambled along, she more than Roger savouring the salty, fishy smell.

'Only the second time I've wandered down this far,' Roger said. 'It's what our American cousins call quaint, I believe.'

'It's the original Fairbourne,' she said, looking up to the two hills in which the place was situated, 'and the stream or bourne now runs under the road.'

His eyes followed her gaze upwards towards the twin hills. 'That's where I usually go, walking on the hills. That's perfect.'

They sauntered as far as the lift that saved people walking the 100 steps to the clifftop then retraced their steps, going back towards the pier and the theatre.

It was very hot for April and they stopped at the kiosk further along and Roger bought two ice creams.

'Reckon Arnold's got it coming to him, the way he's carrying on,' Roger said. 'He's totally out of court, of course. I think Peter will be playing his part soon if he doesn't behave himself.'

Betty said quickly, 'Don't let's talk about it, Roger. It's all so unpleasant.'

He looked down at her, 'All right, we'll speak of nicer things. There's a pianist who plays at one of the hotels on a Sunday evening. He's quite brilliant and I'm going. Want to come?'

'I'd love to. The piano is one of my favourite instruments.'

'Is it? Me too. Do you play?'

'Yes. Not particularly well, but I enjoy it and — ' She stopped herself, she had almost said '*and Lillee loves to dance to the tunes*' but she didn't want to spoil this little interlude.

'It's a date then. Sunday at six outside the Swan Hotel.'

★ ★ ★

Over a drink and a snack she discovered some of Roger's tastes in music. More highbrow than hers and not as catholic but she totally agreed with him that the pianist was one of the best. 'He's a local and does this in his

27

spare time,' he told her, 'but of course he should be more widely heard. He works as a solicitor's clerk during the week and goes around hotels and pubs on Sundays. His talent deserves much more.'

She liked the way he was so positive about everything they discussed. She often doubted her decisions after she had made them and admired his confidence.

The following afternoon she met him on the beach along with several others of the cast, but that was more by accident than design. She had noticed Prince Kingly on the sand near the pier, showing off, singing and conducting his own little musical soirée and, like the others who were there, had laughingly gone down to cheer him on. Nicola and Roger were among the group on the beach, though whether they had gone there together or simply met by accident on seeing the performance she never knew.

Betty wasn't even sure where she wanted the friendship with Roger to go. With so many people in couples and her little daughter away in London with her mother, life was often lonely. Roger was the only man she had been drawn to since Lillee's father Chen had died and she was daring to hope a little.

4

Damn Betty, Crystal thought, as she hurried to Arnold's dressing room a good bit later than usual. She felt cross with the woman for keeping her so long but short of pushing her out of the room there wasn't much she could do without drawing attention to her trysts with Arnold. She realized that her fellow thespians were aware of what was going on, but they couldn't prove it and that was how she wanted it to stay.

Arnold was a long way from being her ideal man, as indeed were most men, including, and especially, her husband Tom. Nevertheless Arnold was the best of the bunch here. She didn't fancy that cocksure little Prince Kingly, nor harsh-faced Roger Johnson, although she admitted to herself that Roger did have a certain Gallic charm. Not her type, though.

Her husband often told her that she was oversexed, but she needed the boost that it gave her and Arnold was rough, eager and willing. Her body tingled with excitement and anticipation as she tapped and simultaneously opened Arnold Brand's dressing room door.

29

She knew that he would be alone; Roger Johnson, with whom he shared the room, always kept out of the way between the matinee and the evening performance.

At first she couldn't see him and she gazed anxiously round the room. From the side of the screen in the corner she saw his sockless foot poking out. It looked as smooth as marble. Totally at odds with the rest of him, she thought mischievously, remembering the artistic body and ruddy complexion. He was a heavy man to fall too; she doubted if she would be able to lift him. She moved into the tiny room and peered round the screen. Arnold Brand was sprawled on the floor, a dark crimson stain covering the enormous tattoo which spread its tentacles across his chest.

★　★　★

Crystal's screams brought Charlie the stage-door keeper, Tim Merry and Nicola Coates. Charlie immediately took charge, his years in the police force giving him superiority over the others.

'Stop screaming, Crystal, and wait in the corridor,' he said, and to Nicola, 'You too, love, and stay with her.'

He got on his knees beside Arnold while

the stage manager ushered the girls out. 'Is he dead, Charlie?' he asked.

'Yes.' Charlie stood up. 'Better phone the police, Tim, and make sure nobody leaves the building. Do you know where everyone is?'

'Of course I don't. There's — there's another hour to go before curtain up.'

'You lock the front of the house and I'll see to the stage door,' Charlie said. 'And while you're phoning, I'll check the rest of the place.'

Looking very shaken, Tim Merry went along to his office to telephone the police.

★ ★ ★

Old Harry pasted the last cancellation notice outside the theatre, and shuffled in again.

'What's up?' he said to Tim Merry, who was hovering nearby. 'Has that bugger Arnold Brand dropped down dead at last?'

Detective Sergeant George Binns, who was walking through the foyer at that moment, heard him. He stopped and asked, 'What makes you think that?'

'Wishful thinking,' the old man replied, and the sergeant walked on and into the manager's office, which Detective Inspector Carding had requisitioned.

'Right,' John Carding said, 'we'll talk to

31

everyone individually and take statements. I've organized the rest of the boys interviewing the stagehands, electricians and what-have-you — we'll take the cast. And we'll start with the one who found him, if they've managed to stop the flood!'

★ ★ ★

Crystal had stopped crying by the time she entered the room. And considering the noisy, distraught sobs that had echoed along the corridor when the policemen arrived, John Carding thought she looked remarkably glamorous. Her shoulder-length golden hair was hanging loosely around her face, and although her baby-blue eyes watered as she looked at him, there was no puffiness beneath or around them. Well, she was an actress, he thought.

'You are Crystal Holman?' he asked when she had sat curvaceously in the chair he indicated.

Lowering her head, she nodded.

'Are you married, Miss Holman?'

The watery look was replaced with one of wariness, but her voice was still hushed as she said, 'What's that got to do with Arnold's m-murder, Inspector?'

He spoke gently and his sergeant listened

and watched the woman intently.

'It may seem irrelevant, Miss Holman, but it helps us a great deal to know all the facts from the beginning. We can find out these things very easily, you know, but it saves time and temper if people volunteer the information.'

'I am married, Inspector. But in show business, you know, you become very, very fond of the people you work with. Arnold — ' She gulped back her distress. 'Arnold and I were — friends.'

'I see.'

'People will tell you that we were more than friends, Inspector, but it isn't true. We have — ' Her eyes filled with tears and she blinked furiously. 'We had a mutual interest, a great passion for the theatre. We . . . '

'I understand, Mrs Holman, and forgive me if I rush you a little but I am sure you want to find Arnold Brand's killer as much as we do. So just two things more, please. Why did you go to Mr Brand's dressing room? And what time was it when you went?'

Crystal hesitated. It was for only a second, but the inspector and his sergeant were aware of it. George Binns made a note on the pad in front of him.

'I'm — I'm not sure of the exact time. I wanted to see Arnold about a change of emphasis we had done during the matinee,' she said. 'I know it sounds silly, but during a run we do try to — to alter our inflections slightly. To improve the performance and stop it getting stale. I — '

Once again Inspector Carding interrupted her. 'When you knocked and there was no reply, how long before you went in?'

'Only a moment.'

'And when you didn't see him immediately, you looked around the room for him?'

Crystal's 'yes' was long and drawn out.

'Did it occur to you that maybe he wasn't in the room? That he might have popped out for a sandwich or something before the next performance?'

She looked across to him then, her eyes widening as she said earnestly, 'Oh no. He never went out between houses.'

'Never?'

She looked him straight in the eye now and said, 'Never, Inspector.'

'Thank you, Mrs Holman. That will be all for the moment, unless of course you recall the time you went to Mr Brand's room. I would like you to stay in the theatre a while longer please as I may want to talk to you again.' He pushed a pad towards her. 'Would you write your name, home address and telephone number here, please?'

'Of course, Inspector, I'll do anything I can, but will it be long before we can leave the theatre?'

'Not long. Will you ask Mr Merry to come in, please?'

He grinned at his sergeant when she had left. 'Wonder what sort of an actress she is?'

'She's the female lead in most of the plays.'

'I think she's a tough cookie, but we'll stick to the gentle approach just now. She's not as devastated as she wants us to believe, is she? Come in,' he called in answer to the light tap on the door.

Tim Merry looked between forty-five and fifty, John Carding thought. There were grey edgings to the sides of his thinning hair, and wrinkle lines on his forehead which suggested he was often worried.

'Sit down, Mr Merry,' the inspector said. 'A nasty business.'

'Yes, yes indeed. I don't know what will happen now.'

'Arnold Brand played an important part, Mr Merry?'

'They all do. He and Crystal are our leads for most of the time, but in these plays with such a small cast — there are only six of them, you know, but he can be replaced. Our ASM — assistant stage manager — is the understudy for all the men.'

'I see. You were one of the first on the scene, I believe, after the discovery? Will you tell us exactly what happened and where everyone was when you arrived?'

Tim rubbed his hands together nervously. 'Well . . . Crystal screamed and it was a — a powerful scream, not a play-acting one, if you see what I mean. An urgent scream. I rushed along the corridor to see what was happening. Arnold's dressing room door was partly open and Crystal was in there, still screaming. I almost bumped into Charlie — he's the stage-door keeper and an ex-policeman — and, well, that's about it, really. I rang for the police.'

'You didn't try to revive him? You knew he was dead?'

'Charlie crouched down beside him and said he was dead and not to touch anything. We got the girls outside in the corridor and — Oh yes, we locked the theatre front and back.'

'Girls, you said. Was someone there with Crystal?' the inspector asked.

'Yes, Nicola. Nicola Coates. She's in the play.'

'And what time was this, Mr Merry?'

'The curtain came down at ten past five. About quarter past six, I think. I — I'm afraid I didn't really notice.'

'Thank you very much, Mr Merry.' He pushed the pad towards him. 'If we might have your full name, home address and telephone number, please, in case we want to get in touch later.'

Sergeant Binns made a note on his pad to the effect that Tim Merry was left-handed.

The stage manager had just reached the door when, recalling his sergeant's exchange with the bill poster, Inspector Carding said, 'Mr Merry, was Arnold Brand a popular member of the cast?'

Tim Merry turned back. 'Popular? No. No, I can't in truth say he was popular.'

'Why?'

'Well, it's not for me to . . . to sit in judgement on my fellow men.' Some of the wrinkles on his forehead disappeared into his hair.

'But you must have an opinion about it, Mr Merry. In your job you see them all from a third person view really, don't you? And in such a small team . . .'

'He created an unhappy atmosphere.'

'Were they all his enemies, or could you pinpoint one?'

'No-one liked him much. Except — except Crystal, of course.'

'Were they lovers?'

'Oh, now I — I . . . I don't know much

about their private lives, Inspector. And I — I try not to listen to gossip.'

'No matter. Have you worked with Arnold Brand before?'

'Once,' he said.

'And was that an unhappy experience too?'

'Yes, it was.'

'Why?'

'Well, it was some years ago now, Inspector, but I've never forgotten it because one of the young actresses committed suicide.' He took his hand from the doorknob and pressed it against the other one as though he were unconsciously saying his prayers. 'Not because of Arnold, you understand. It was just one of those unhappy coincidences that this tragedy happened during that particular run.'

'Can you remember the verdict on the actress?' Carding's voice was deceptively gentle.

Tim Merry shook his head. 'No. I never went to the inquest or anything. It — it didn't happen in the theatre so I don't really know.'

When Tim Merry had left the room, Inspector Carding swivelled his chair round. 'Well, George, what d'you think?' he said.

'People don't get snopped because they create an unhappy atmosphere, chief. When do we see his wife, and brokenhearted

Crystal's husband?'

'When we've finished here.' The phone on the desk rang and Sergeant Binns answered it.

'Yes. OK. I've got that. Thanks, Fred.'

Turning to his boss he said, 'They've got the bullet; it's a round-nosed one from a pistol and Fred says the ones that used those were Lugers.'

Carding made a note on the pad. 'Interesting,' he said.

The remaining four in the cast contributed little to the picture. Betty Morse and Nicola Coates shared a dressing room. Both in their early twenties, they were as unalike as could be. Betty was tall, dark haired and had burning brown eyes 'which could do devastating things to a man', according to George. 'If you like that kind of brooding beauty,' he added. Nicola was just five feet tall, with fair skin, corn-coloured hair and a fragility that made Sergeant Binns say afterwards, 'Blimey, is she real? She's like a beautiful china doll.'

'Mmm. She was also one of the first on the scene.'

Roger Johnson, who shared the dressing room with the murdered actor, was in his late twenties. He was tall and lean, with a mobile face which seemed to change shape several times during his interview.

'No, I didn't care for Arnold Brand much,' he said in answer to that question. 'Thought a deal too much of himself.'

Roger had gone out between performances and had a cup of tea and a bun at the cafe opposite the stage door. 'The first I knew of the murder was when I tried to get in again and the panic bolts were in place.'

'Panic bolts, Mr Johnson?'

'They're pushed over to stop people getting in but can be opened from the inside, of course. Stage doors are never locked while the theatre is open,' he added patronizingly.

'Thank you, Mr Johnson. Did you see anyone enter or leave the stage door when you were in the cafe?'

'No. I was sitting in the back. You would only be able to see from the tables near the entrance.'

Prince Kingly came in next. 'Prince — is that your real name or your stage name?' Carding asked him.

The actor hummed and hawed a bit before revealing his real name to be Joe Smith. 'But I wouldn't want everyone to know, Superintendent.'

'Inspector.'

'Inspector. You know, in this business images are so important. Joe Smith just doesn't have the ring of stardom about it that

Prince Kingly does. And I didn't murder Arnold.'

They left Charlie Ferguson until last. He had retired four years previously from the police force and moved down to the south coast because his wife had relatives there. Because the theatre was his absorbing passion, he had applied for a job as stage-door keeper when the amateur drama group he was part of folded.

'Gives me enough free time to satisfy the wife,' he said, 'and I enjoy the job.'

'Nobody seems to have liked Brand much, but who hated him enough to murder? Is there anything you've noticed that would help, Charlie?'

'No, Inspector, but I can fill you in on some of the background they may not tell you,' he said. 'Crystal was his girlfriend — I think only since this play. She's married to a writer, Tom Holman. She always spent the time between matinee and second house in Arnold's dressing room. Roger, who shared it, used to make himself scarce. He's sweet on Betty who shares with Nicola.'

'So Crystal and Prince have a room to themselves, and the others share?'

'That's right. Betty and Nicola together, and Arnold and Roger.'

'So why didn't Brand go to Crystal's room?

41

Would have saved a lot of swapping.'

Charlie said, 'I've often wondered that and the only thing I can come up with is that he's afraid of her husband coming in and finding them. I've only seen Tom Holman once, but he's a big strapping bloke. Must be nearly six foot — and muscular. Looks more like a boxer than a writer.'

* * *

Back at police headquarters, Sergeant Binns typed up his notes. Someone brought in the late edition of the local evening paper.

'Actor murdered,' it said in huge type across the front page. 'Arnold Brand, who was appearing in *The Swapping Party*, a play involved with wife-swapping and murder, was found shot in his dressing room one hour before he was due on stage for the evening performance.'

'Probably the most publicity he's had for years,' he muttered to himself. He pulled the pad with the suspects' names and addresses on towards him. Graphology was one of his hobbies. The inspector knew this and always asked his interviewees to write down their own details. Not that they officially used the information, but it often gave pointers.

Sergeant Binns had studied the subject for

a good many years now and always stressed to his superior that to do a good job you needed to use it in conjunction with other knowledge.

Of course, these people were all under a certain amount of strain at the moment, and this would probably be reflected in their handwriting. The policeman in him acknowledged that innocent folk often lied because of something else in their lives which they would rather not be generally known. This factor always clouded an enquiry.

Binns would have liked more — at least half a page. He would also have preferred a letter or text rather than a name and address. Nevertheless he could discover a little of each personality from these samples.

He noted the bold right-hand slant of Prince Kingly's effort. Definitely an extrovert character here — simply meeting the man bore that out. Ambition was there too in the large upper loops of part of his address. Sergeant Binns smiled to himself as he recalled the man addressing Inspector Carding as Superintendent. Ingratiating, cocky little man, he thought. He doesn't know our John Carding — he would have swiftly had him taped.

Some anxiety was shown in all of the writing but the one that revealed the most stress was Tim, the stage-manager. Sergeant Binns studied the sample for several minutes. All the signs of worry and strain were there in the formation and slant of his letters and the heavy filling in of the loops. It tied in with his performance when being interviewed, but was this because the man was a natural worrier with a lot of responsibility, or because he had a specific problem connected to the murder of one of his cast?

5

A brilliant blue sky penetrated the delicate greenery of the trees in Sloane Avenue the following day when Sergeant Binns and his inspector called on Arnold Brand's widow.

'She took the news of her husband's murder stoically, according to the two police officers who broke it to her,' the inspector said. 'But from what we learned at the theatre yesterday he seemed to be playing the field. On the other hand, she's a well-known actress and this may have helped her cope with the news initially.'

'Yes, I suppose it could have.' The sergeant was looking at the imposing and elegant house. 'Nice place.' he murmured. 'He couldn't have been doing too badly.'

The door of the Tudor-style house was opened by a fair-haired woman.

'Mrs Brand?' the inspector queried softly.

She nodded. 'Please come in,' she said. 'It's about Arnold, isn't it?'

'Yes. I'm sorry to worry you at this difficult time, Mrs Brand, but there are questions which possibly only you could answer.'

He sat down awkwardly on a brown dralon

settee. 'We won't detain you longer than necessary.'

'That's all right. I'm — not going anywhere for some hours yet, Inspector,' she answered, humour showing briefly in her eyes.

George Binns winced at his chief's choice of words. John Carding had a reputation at the station for obtaining more information, with his gentle manner, than many who had a brisk, efficient-sounding approach, but his lapses into police language, often at the wrong moment, were notorious.

Iris Brand was fragile looking, soft hair framing a heart-shaped face, grey eyes luminous yet not showing signs that she had cried all night, as George Binns mentally noted. Never surprised at his chief's tactics, he listened with interest as John Carding said enthusiastically, 'I've seen you many times on stage, Mrs Brand, and admired you greatly. Strange, but you seem much taller from an audience distance.'

'I am taller on stage, Inspector.'

She didn't enlarge on her statement, but sat opposite him with her hands folded together in her lap.

George Binns quietly made notes as his inspector took her through the usual probing questions about her late husband. Did he have any known enemies? Was their marriage happy? Was anyone jealous of his success?

She answered him quietly, only hesitating on the happiness of her marriage.

'You can be absolutely frank with me,' Inspector Carding pressed, 'and my sergeant is the soul of discretion too. Was your husband involved with another woman, Mrs Brand?' She shivered suddenly. 'I need to check everything, Mrs Brand. I shall soon find out, so better perhaps for you to tell me what you know.'

'He usually had an affair with the leading lady wherever he was working,' she said hesitantly, looking up and into his face properly for the first time since the interview began. 'I don't know if he and Crystal Holman were lovers — I imagine they were.'

★ ★ ★

'One thing puzzles me, chief,' George said when they were in the car again and on their way to see Crystal's husband, Tom Holman. 'There were a lot of people about, including the backstage staff, yet no-one seemed to hear the shot.'

'I take your point, George. If Crystal's screams were enough to bring everyone there rushing to the scene, a gunshot almost certainly would. Unless it was mistaken for a car backfiring. But no-one mentioned the sound in any connection so I would think a silencer of some sort was used. And the muffled sort of sound they make probably wouldn't be noticed or even heard outside the room. It means it was a planned job, of course. It's important because it gave the murderer time to get clear. In theory the murderer had an hour between shows, but less than half that time in reality because of Crystal's regular trysts. Which the rest of the cast, and every back-stage electrician and carpenter knew about. Next road on the left, I believe, George.'

Tom Holman answered the door himself. In his mid thirties, he was, as Charlie Ferguson had told them, a big, strapping bloke. He took them into his large study. Three walls, including the one by his desk, were lined with books, and the desk itself, leather topped and with drawers either side, held a typewriter, a dictionary, thesaurus and a pile of scrap paper neatly clipped together. The fourth wall seemed to have disappeared behind the largest poster of guns either of them had ever seen. In the centre of the room were three brown leather armchairs.

'What can I do for you?' Tom Holman did not ask either of them to sit down although he walked behind his desk and rested his enormous hands on the dark red top, before settling himself into the comfortable-looking office chair behind it.

'Did you know Arnold Brand, Mr Holman?'

'Aye, I knew 'im.'

'How well did you know him? Did you like him?' Inspector Carding could be as curt as he was gentle when the occasion warranted, and Sergeant Binns permitted himself an inward grin as these two matched up. He knew his superior would be riled by such discourteous treatment.

'Not well, and, no, I didn't like him. Now can I get back to work?'

'Certainly, after a few more questions, Mr Holman. It was your wife who discovered the murder and I imagine you want it cleared up as quickly as possible too.'

'Makes no odds to me. Crystal didn't shoot him, if that's what you're thinking.'

'How do you know?'

'I asked her. She's a flighty bitch most of the time, but she usually tells me the truth.'

'Did she tell you that she and Arnold Brand were having an affair?'

'Didn't need to. I knew. Look, Inspector, I'm a busy man and I'd like to get on. Neither Crystal nor I killed Arnold Brand so you're wasting your time here.'

Inspector Carding walked across to the

wall covered by the gun poster. Beneath each picture were the details of the weapon.

'I see you have your research close at hand,' he said.

'Yes.'

'Specializing in crime?'

'In westerns.'

'Do you own a gun?'

'No.'

'So you specialize in westerns, Mr Holman. Do you write anything else?'

Tom Holman stood up suddenly. 'No, though what that has to do with investigating a murder beats me. If you think that writing westerns makes me a suspicious character you must be hard up.'

John Carding chose to ignore the man's rude manner for the moment. He hadn't finished. 'Where were you between 3.30 and 6.30 last night, Mr Holman?'

'Where I am now.' He walked past them towards the door.

'Is there anyone who can prove that?'

'You know damn well there isn't.'

'So in theory, you could have driven to the theatre, killed Arnold Brand and driven home again without anyone knowing you had left this house?'

'Yes. Except that I didn't. Ask anyone in the theatre, that stage-door chappie who watches everybody like a hawk. You won't find a soul who saw me because I wasn't there. I was here as I just told you.'

★ ★ ★

'We shall be talking to Tom Holman again,' John Carding said fifteen minutes later when they were ensconced in what was probably his local.

'He wouldn't need a gun — he'd probably use his strength.'

'He had a motive, George.'

'You mean Crystal and Arnold?'

'Mmm. But I would have thought he'd have warned him off — big macho bloke like that. According to Charlie, that's why they used his dressing room instead of hers. I don't imagine that would have been a deterrent anyway. Tom Holman would have sussed them out if he had to. Did you get the idea that he wasn't bothered about Crystal's extra-marital affairs as long as he was left to get on in peace? Or do you think that's simply what he wanted us to believe?'

'Really didn't care, I think. Wonder if that's his usual attitude, brisk to the point of rudeness, or if he doesn't want us probing too deeply? You know, chief, most writers are friendlier than that towards us.'

'Not a reading man myself — except for the papers and car manuals. But he'd know a bit about guns, I suppose, and could probably get hold of one in the interests of 'research.' Had a goodly collection on that poster too.'

'Yes, sir, but not a Luger, I noticed.'

Inspector Carding smiled. 'Quite so, George. I don't think they used them in the old Wild West. We'll check his gun licence. He may be lying about not owning a gun. There was an iota of hesitation in his voice. Let's get back and see if anything more has cropped up. By the way, the inquest is fixed for four weeks time.'

He returned the glasses to the bar, which wasn't as crowded as when they came in, and Sergeant Binns watched him having a chat with the barman.

'Anything doing, chief?' he asked when they were outside again.

'Not sure, but Tom Holman comes in about three times a week, and just recently Arnold Brand has been frequenting the place too.'

'Together?'

'He wouldn't commit himself. Says he's usually busy but he thought he'd seen them drinking together on a couple of occasions.'

Back at the station the report on the weapon was waiting. It told them no more than they already knew from the post mortem; that the bullet was from a German Luger, fired through a soft shield to deaden the noise, and that the gun had not yet been found.

'Look, you go to the theatre tonight, George, and have a chat with Charlie while the play's on and everyone else is occupied. The theatre is open for business again. Get the lowdown on the cast's private lives. OK?'

'OK, chief. Will you be at home if anything spectacular crops up?'

'Yes. Ruth has people in for supper and I promised I'd try and keep the evening free.' He pulled a face. 'See you tomorrow, George.'

★ ★ ★

George visited the front of the Victoriana theatre first, and mingled with the crowds in the foyer. There was a queue at the box office marked 'For Tonight's Performance', and as he watched, the 'Sold Out' notices went up. Macabre lot, the public, he thought. Flocking to see the play now because of the murder, no doubt. He walked thoughtfully down the half dozen steps to the pavement, along the road and round the corner until he came to the stage door. There was a single light illuminating the words and he pushed the bars and went in.

Charlie was in the cubbyhole reading the evening paper.

'Evening, Charlie.'

'Evening. Oh, it's you, Sergeant. How's it going then?'

'Can't complain. You busy, Charlie?'

The stage-doorman folded the paper neatly and tucked it away. 'No, not until the fans come round after the show.' He looked at his watch. 'They'll all be in now — only two minutes to curtain up.'

'The sold out notices went up just now,' George said.

'I'm not surprised. Been playing to half-empty houses until the murder. Now it's drawing them in.'

'Who is playing Arnold Brand's part, Charlie?'

'Peter Strong. He's the assistant stage manager and understudies them all. The company doesn't run to one each. Not many this size do. He does the men and Doris Wiggs, the dresser, does the women.'

'Mmm. Tim Merry mentioned him last night. Don't recall seeing him, though. Where was he?'

'Off sick.'

'What was wrong with him?'

54

'Bad migraine. He gets 'em sometimes. He spoke to Tim in the morning and rang me half an hour before the matinee to check everyone was there. Said he felt much better but was glad he hadn't got to face the lights. He's here now, of course, playing Arnold's part.'

'I take it he could get into the theatre without anyone questioning him if he wanted to?' George Binns asked.

'I suppose so. Yes, I can see what you're getting at, but he wasn't here on Wednesday, I'd swear to that. He'd have to come past me, see — unless he was in the audience, of course.'

'Got his address?'

Charlie took a book from the shelf and thumbed through it. 'Here it is.' He wrote the address down and handed it over. 'You could see him after the show tonight,' he said.

'No, I'll leave it to the chief. What I need is a bit of background on a couple of people, Charlie.'

'Fire away, Sarge. It's a nasty business, and although I didn't care for Arnold much I'd like to see his murderer caught.'

'Right. Apart from the pretty general feeling of dislike by almost everyone for him, who carried it on to murder? Can we talk a bit about the chap who shared his dressing room? Roger something . . . '

'Roger Johnson. Strange you should mention him because he sometimes goes to Betty
and Nicola's room between performances on
matinee days. Not always, just now and then.
Usually with a bundle of books under his arm
so I don't think it's for the same reason as
Crystal's visit to Arnold. I think both girls
have a soft spot for Roger but he's an
uncommitted type. What I'd call a gentle flirt,
really, you know, safety in numbers. I've seen
him several times chatting up the waitress in
the cafe over the road too. Well, he's young
and fancy-free, I suppose.'

'Go on,' George said.

'Nicola and Betty share a dressing room
and Nicola goes out when Roger pays a visit.
Most unhappy she is about it too, although
she tries not to show it. Sitting here, you
know, you see more of the real person than
most. Once they are in their dressing rooms
they become actors and actresses, but this
little passage between the street and the stage
is often a transitional place. Sometimes you
can feel them shrug off their own personality
and put on the mask.'

'Did you never want to act yourself,
Charlie? You're obviously so keen on the
business.'

'Did a bit of amateur dramatics when I was

in the force. Always been involved on the fringe, so to speak, same as my dad before me, but I'd never have made the grade enough to earn a regular living. You're right, though, I do love the theatre, and this job suits me fine. I'm part of the team — not that this lot have a happy team. There's a lot of undercurrents, but they're stuck with each other for the summer season.'

'And I gather they do a different play every week?'

'That's right. Change on a Thursday so the fortnight visitors can see a new programme. It was the last night of *The Swapping Party* when Arnold copped it. For four weeks, anyway — then they do 'em all through again.'

George left half an hour later. 'Thanks, Charlie. I'll be in again. No need to ask you to keep your eyes peeled — it's second nature once you've hitched your wagon to the force, isn't it?'

★   ★   ★

Sergeant Binns filled his inspector in about his evening at the theatre the next day.

'The two girls who share a room, Nicola and Betty, don't get on. A bit of a love tussle with Roger Johnson apparently. And Prince

Kingly used to go around with Crystal at one time, but not since they've been here. He's married, but not to anyone in showbiz, and he doesn't often go home. Fancies himself as a bit of a matinee idol. Charlie thinks he has a bit of skirt here in Fairbourne. Tim Merry, according to Charlie, is heading for an ulcer. Too much of a worrier over everything, he says, but the pièce de résistance is that the understudy was off sick yesterday.'

'So he wasn't interviewed with the rest?'

'That's about it.'

'Mmm, we slipped up there, George. Tim Merry mentioned him — he's also the assistant stage manager.'

'I've got his address, chief. I didn't see him last night, I left before the show finished.'

'I'll get one of the boys on to it.'

'How did you get on, chief? Nice supper party?'

'As a matter of fact, it proved very interesting. Our friends know better than to discuss with me any particular news item, but they couldn't resist murder on their doorstep — especially when it was an actor they had seen in the play last week!'

'Any inside knowledge?'

'Iris Brand, the late lamented's widow — she's billed as Iris Masters, by the way — is a terrific actress. I knew that, of course

— I've seen her several times. According to our friends she was afraid of her husband, who swept her off her feet when she was very young — sixteen or seventeen, they thought — and he was twenty-four. Also, and again I am quoting, she is grander, more flamboyant, and has the confidence she lacks offstage once she sets foot on the boards. All this they learned from a friend whose friend is Iris Brand's greatest friend.'

George smiled. 'Bit involved, chief.'

'I know. Still, she wouldn't be the first actress to hide her personality behind a character, would she? And from what I saw of her the other day, I can believe it's true. They also said she knew about his little affairs and ignored them, which ties in with what she told us. But something she didn't tell us, George, is that she has recently acquired a boyfriend herself. His name is Rob. And at that point their knowledge finished. Damned annoying, that, but we should have his surname within the hour. If not we'll ask her, though I'd prefer a surprise visit to him. According to my informants, she has been with him a few months.'

'Is he an actor or what, chief?'

'No idea at the moment. They only knew his Christian name, which she had apparently mentioned. No more. Shouldn't be too

59

difficult to trace though.'

'Right, chief, when do we interview Rob?'

'When do *you* interview Rob, you mean? Today, George, just as soon as I've got his surname and address for you. They're working on it at the desk.'

6

It took longer than they expected to find a name and address for Iris Brand's boyfriend so Sergeant George Binns busied himself with some of the routine work that had piled up while he'd been involved in the Arnold Brand case. The part about police life he liked least was the paperwork.

Rob, full name Robert Paul Mantle, turned out to be an actor.

'How come we've not heard of him, chief?'

'He's not exactly a household name. Just a small-part player.' John Carding consulted his notes. 'He is currently appearing in *The Bedside Lamp* at Worthing. He's probably at home now — there isn't a matinee today. See what you can unearth, George.'

★ ★ ★

It was a pleasant drive along the coast to Worthing and George Binns appreciated the change. He parked the car, checked his street map once more, then set off towards the promenade, noticing the wealthy-looking houses and thinking to himself that there must still be money about.

Robert Mantle lived in a neat flat within a small block just off the seafront.

'I'm renting it for the summer season,' he said. 'I prefer my own place whenever I can.'

Tall, with light ginger hair, a fair complexion and eyes that seemed to change from hazel to green with astonishing rapidity, Rob admitted he was in love with the murdered man's widow.

'Met her through a friend who was in the same play last year,' he said. 'He took me to her dressing room and we hit it off right away.'

'And you've been seeing her ever since?'

'More or less. Several of us went for a meal after the show, and quite simply I fell in love.'

'Did you know then that she was married?'

'Yes, I did. But it was an unhappy partnership — that was general knowledge among her group — so I felt no compunction about giving her a good time.'

'Is that all it was, or were you hoping it would lead to a more permanent liaison, Mr Mantle?'

Rob twisted his face into a theatrical grimace. 'I should have anticipated that question, shouldn't I? The truthful answer is yes. Maybe not immediately but quite early into our relationship. The more I saw and heard about the situation, the more I wanted to protect her. I didn't kill him, though. I was working that afternoon and evening, over here in Worthing, and was at the theatre until the curtain came down just after ten o'clock that night.'

'You aren't married, Mr Mantle?'

'No.'

Sergeant Binns rose to leave and, taking a leaf out of his boss's book, said in a casual way, 'Any girlfriends before Mrs Brand?'

Rob stood up too, almost dwarfing the burly sergeant. His fists were clenched and his tone was sharp now. 'Of course.'

'But you were free when you and Mrs Br — '

'She likes to be known as Iris Masters, Sergeant, and to answer your rather impertinent question, I was an uncommitted man prior to our meeting. I did take girls out right up to meeting her, but she's been the only one since. I can't be straighter than that with you.'

★ ★ ★

Reporting back later, George told Inspector Carding, 'He says they are deeply in love. He knew she was married but very unhappily so. Bit of an idealist, I'd say, wanting to rescue

63

the fairy princess from the dragon. He gave what sounded like honest answers to my questions and he did it in a no-nonsense sort of manner.'

'Is he married?'

'No, but he gave up other women when Iris came on the scene.'

'Would you put Robert Mantle on the list of suspects?'

'Not sure, chief. He was pretty worked up about Iris. Fiery when roused, I'd say. If, and I'm using supposition now, Brand refused to divorce her, I should think Rob would feel angry enough to go and see him. The sun, moon and stars shine from her eyes for him — that much was obvious.'

'But Charlie would have known if he'd been in, and we do know the murder took place between 5.10 and 6.30, but more probably between 5.15 — which gives Arnold time to get back to his dressing room — and 5.35, because Crystal usually went to him within twenty minutes of coming off, and the murderer would want to be out of the way by then, unless of course Crystal is the killer!'

'Arnold had no change of clothes to do — his tie was on the dressing table near the mirror. The shirt and jacket he wore in the final scene of the play were on a hanger on the rail, and he was in his underpants only.

That would only take five minutes. The murderer came in, probably talked to him while he went to wash his hands and shot him as he turned back from the basin. That would go along with the position in which he was found, sprawled on his back on the floor. The tiny washbasin is behind the screen anyway. Or it could be that the murderer came in while Brand was the other side of it and the assassin appeared round the screen as he turned round.'

'Right . . . Either of them means the victim didn't have a chance. But I believe he would have changed, George. If he and Crystal were going to have a tumble he'd never have kept his stage clothes on, even if they weren't period gear. From my scant knowledge of theatricals, they usually look after their costumes. He was probably going to put on a pair of jeans and a T-shirt after their little peccadillo, so the killer had to strike quickly before Crystal Holman appeared on the scene.'

George pursed his lips and made a sucking sound. 'Which means he was shot within ten minutes of taking his bow.'

'I'd say it was likely. He was obviously changing because he had no vest or shirt on, just his underpants. It also presumes that he was killed by someone who knew his habits.

And outside of the cast and maybe some of the behind-the-scenes staff, the killer would not know he was to be found alone in his dressing room within that rather limited timescale.'

'It narrows it down, chief.'

Carding paced the room. 'It certainly does. The other scenario is that the killer was already in the room waiting for the right moment. Not a lot of places to hide in those dressing rooms, but not an impossible task either.'

'You would still need to know he was going to be there, and if it was someone from outside, they'd need to get past Charlie.' Sergeant Binns spoke quietly now. 'It was a well-planned murder, whichever way you look at it.'

'If one of them goes sick or missing it would make our work much easier,' the inspector said. 'Meanwhile, any one of them could be responsible, as indeed could someone coming in off the street. The murdered man had a lot of enemies, but so far no strong motive for this particular killing has emerged in my mind.'

George nodded in agreement. 'They are all very much on their guard at present, sir, but if one of the cast is involved the tension will surely grow worse and give us a lead.'

Inspector Carding reached up and scratched his head in a distracted fashion. 'I hope you're right, George. I do hope you're right.'

* * *

John Carding was at the theatre when Crystal arrived for the evening performance.

'Just a few things I'd like to check, Mrs Holman. I won't keep you long,' he said.

'But, Inspector, couldn't it wait until after the show?'

He ignored the pleading in her voice and eyes. 'It won't take long,' he repeated. 'Now we know that you always went to Arnold Brand's dressing room on matinee days and spent the time between first and second house with him. Were you your usual time on the evening of his murder?'

She winced and lowered her eyes. 'It's too awful, Inspector. I still can't believe it, you know.'

He inclined his head and said sympathetically, 'It must be very difficult for you, Mrs Holman, but I'm sorry you did not trust us enough to be honest in the first place. Now, were you later than usual that particular evening?'

Her high-pitched voice sounded squeaky as she nodded and said, 'Yes, I was a little later than usual. You seem to know a lot about us. Charlie, I suppose. Doesn't miss much, that one. Or Nicola or Betty? No,' she went on, 'Nicola's too timid, no spunk, but Betty might. Was it Betty or Charlie who told you about me sometimes going to Arnold's dressing room?'

'The theatre grapevine is like the police grapevine, I imagine, Mrs Holman — in a word, efficient. The main point is that we do know you and Arnold Brand were lovers. The morality of it doesn't concern me, but the fact that Arnold was murdered between the matinee and the evening performance does.'

'Oh, In-inspector.' She burst into noisy sobs.

'Come now,' he said, suddenly impatient, 'don't let us waste time, Mrs Holman. How much later than usual were you in going to Arnold Brand's dressing room, and why were you later? What held you up?'

His change of tone had the desired effect and Crystal held on to her control and answered quietly, 'Betty came in.'

'What did she want?'

'To return some books I'd lent Roger.'

'Why didn't Roger return them himself?'

'Because he'd passed them on to Betty to read, I suppose. They are friends — more than friends, as you have possibly deduced

68

from your irrelevant questioning.' She sounded exasperated.

Inspector Carding ignored her rudeness and said calmly, 'So Betty returned the books to you and not to Roger Johnson — that should only have taken a few moments. According to my information you were at least twenty minutes later than usual.'

'Really, Inspector.' She sighed theatrically. 'We talked.'

'What about?'

'Oh, this is ridiculous.' Her blue eyes flashed and her cheeks grew pinker. 'I can't remember. Idle chit-chat. Woman's talk. Nothing important. But she didn't simply come in, lay down the books and disappear. We chatted — behaved in a normal manner. Oh, I'm sorry, you are only doing your job, I suppose, but it seems pointless to me that you keep on about something so trivial as what we talked about in a few idle minutes when Arnold was probably being murdered right then. Surely you ought to be checking on who was in *his* room at that particular time.'

'We are, Mrs Holman, and never fear, we shall find out. I'll leave you now, but should you think of anything you feel may help at all, I'm sure you will let me know immediately, won't you?' It sounded like a softly voiced threat.

'Yes, Inspector, of course. But I don't see how I can.' Her eyes widened appealingly as she said with a sob in her voice, 'I loved Arnold and I want his murderer caught as much as you do.'

★ ★ ★

John Carding went home for an hour. 'Have to go out again later,' he said to his wife, 'but I shouldn't be too late.'

'Oh, darling, must you?'

'Afraid so, my dear. I want to talk to the cast at the Victoriana when they finish tonight.'

Ruth Carding knew better than to suggest it wait until morning. 'Mind how you go,' she said with a smile.

In fact he returned to the theatre that night not to talk to the entire cast but to two members only — Nicola Coates and Betty Morse.

★ ★ ★

Nicola looked pale without her makeup. She answered his questions in a quiet, cultured voice, but with a hint of nervousness. She said she had been in the corridor looking for Vicky, the theatre cat, when Crystal screamed.

70

'Did you go into Arnold Brand's room?'

'No. I started to but Charlie stopped me. I — I took Crystal out into the corridor and a few minutes later Tim Merry came out and said, 'He's dead.''

'How did you get on with Arnold Brand, Miss Coates?'

'I never had much to do with him, Inspector.'

'But you were all in the play. You rehearsed together and acted together. So I will repeat my question; how did you get on with the murdered man, Miss Coates?'

His tone had the desired effect and she said quietly, 'I didn't like him.'

'Why?'

'He was too loud, too full of himself and he caused arguments.'

'Arguments with or about you, Miss Coates?'

Nicola looked uncomfortable, as though she hadn't meant to say as much.

'With Tim Merry mostly. Arnold didn't like taking orders. He wasn't a good team player really, Inspector.'

'There were six of you in the company and for this play you were divided into couples. You partnered Roger Johnson, I believe?'

She nodded.

'And you, Miss Morse, partnered Arnold Brand?'

Betty Morse turned from the dressing table where she had been brushing her hair.

'That is correct, Inspector, and to forestall your next question, we got along quite well.'

'Offstage as well as on?'

She turned sharply. 'We never met outside of the theatre,' she said.

'I believe you went to Crystal Holman's room on the day of the murder,' he said to her. 'Why?'

'Why?' Her eyes, seductive as dark chocolate, seemed to pierce his face. 'To return some books.'

'Books you had borrowed?'

'Yes.'

'How long were you there?' He saw her tense up but she recovered her composure quickly as she repeated his question.

'How long? I don't know. Five or ten minutes, I suppose.'

'And what did you talk about during that time?'

'I . . . can't remember,' she said. 'Probably the play — or the books.' She shrugged and stood up. 'You see, I didn't expect to have to account for my words, Inspector.'

There was a scratching sound at the dressing room door and Nicola walked over and opened it to admit a tabby cat. Picking it up, she cuddled it, and Inspector Carding reached out a hand to stroke it too.

'This is the cat you were looking for when you heard Crystal scream, I presume?'

'Yes, Inspector. I . . . I was worried about her. She usually comes in during the matinee and is waiting when I get back, but I hadn't seen her for several hours.'

Betty walked by. 'If you have finished questioning me, Inspector, I'll get away,' she said pointedly.

'Of course.' He opened the door for her and she went through without either looking at him or thanking him.

'I expect you'd like to get home too,' he said to Nicola. 'May I give you a lift?'

She looked embarrassed. 'No, thank you, Inspector — I have to feed Vicky.' She smiled at him and it transformed her, suddenly making her seem more confident. 'I always feed her after the show — she depends on me now.'

'What did she do before you came?' he said.

'Oh, I think Charlie always made sure she had food and milk, but she took to me and I've been seeing to her since we've been here.'

'What does your roommate feel about sharing with a cat? She didn't look ecstatic when the animal came into the room just now.'

Nicola smiled for the second time since he had met her. 'No, she isn't a cat lover, but there are certain things I'm very determined about. Cats are one, and anyway Betty isn't here for long.'

'Are you?'

'Not really. Long enough to feed Vicky, and I sometimes stay and pet her a little afterwards.'

'I would have thought a pretty girl like you would have a boyfriend waiting to whisk her off somewhere.'

Nicola smiled again. 'Maybe I'm not interested. In any case, there aren't any stage-door Johnnies these days, Inspector. The men and boys who hang around now are a different breed.'

'But you have a boyfriend?'

'No.'

He moved towards the door, pausing to stroke the cat in her arms once more. 'I heard that you and Roger Johnson — Maybe I got that wrong?'

She flushed. 'No, Inspector. I did go out with him a couple of times but he preferred . . . '

'Yes?'

'Other more sophisticated women.'

'Such as Betty Morse?'

She looked startled.

'Well?'

'Betty has — does go out with Roger sometimes, yes.'

He left her still holding the cat and went out to his car, saying a brief good night to Charlie as he went past his little domain.

★ ★ ★

Back home he settled down at the dining room table with a beer, a large sheet of paper and a pencil. Here he listed the names of his suspects, leaving a large space beside each one. Then he filled in his thoughts about each person. Just over an hour later, when Ruth came in with a mug of steaming Ovaltine — 'How you can drink this stuff all year round I don't know,' she said affectionately — he had in front of him an empty glass and a sheet of paper covered with neat notes against each name.

He smiled at her as he folded the paper and a fleeting thought went through his mind. I wonder what George would make of my handwriting? He probably analyzed it long ago.

Picking up the bedtime drink, he glanced across to his wife and said, 'I'll sleep on that little lot tonight, Ruth. Maybe a common denominator will emerge. At the moment I'm

75

baffled. With them all being actors and actresses it makes our job harder. It's not like dealing with ordinary people. You can usually tell when they're concealing something. You can tell when they are acting too — well, most of the time you can — but when you have a bunch who earn their living by acting it's much more difficult. Most of them aren't well documented either because they're not famous. The one most written about is Iris, the murdered man's wife.'

'Yes, even I've heard of her.'

'She didn't broadcast the fact that she was married to Brand,' he said. 'If she had this murder would be headline news and then we'd be inundated with stuff. That's not always useful. Maybe we'll go to the play incognito tomorrow, and I'll study them all from the other side of the footlights. Do you fancy a night at the theatre, my love?'

'Good idea. Now drink up and come to bed. Tomorrow is another day, John.'

7

'Right, George,' Inspector Carding said to his sergeant at the station the following morning, 'have you come up with any of your famous hunches on the Victoriana murder?'

'No, chief. Have you?'

'Not a hunch exactly; don't believe in them. I leave that sort of stuff to you. I do have a strong feeling that we must find out why Betty went to Crystal's room and spent at least twenty minutes talking to her though. She said it was ten but according to Nicola she was gone 'around twenty minutes or so'. What did they talk about? It's codswallop that they small-talked for that length of time. Crystal always went along to Arnold's room within a quarter of an hour of the curtain coming down. I've checked this out with several of the cast, and it seems pretty well known. All right, maybe she was just going when Betty arrived to return the borrowed books, but why did she let her hold her up for so long? I'm thinking aloud now, George, but doesn't it strike you that it must have been something pretty important?'

'Put like that — yes.'

'Look, ring Tim Merry, will you, and tell him I'd like to see all the cast in the theatre this afternoon at three.'

'Right, chief.'

'Then go and see Iris Brand again, and call in at the pub at lunchtime and get talking to some of the locals — I want to find out a bit about Brand's financial status. Of course, his wife's earnings could have paid for that house, but there's a little niggle in my mind, George.'

'Blackmail, chief?'

'It's possible. And get the boys on to that suicide — Gloria Welsh the girl's name was. I've checked with Tim Merry and as far as he can recall it was five years ago, so start looking around then. The play was a comedy called *Lads and Lassies* — the girl had only a small part and he thinks they were at Oxford when it happened. Obviously you'll check to see if any of the ones down here were in it too.'

'Of course, chief,' George said, grinning to himself as he went through the door.

It was a busy morning and John Carding sent out for coffee and sandwiches at quarter past two while he finished tidying up various papers that had been waiting for his attention for the last few days. At twenty minutes to three he strode through the station. 'I'll be at the theatre if something urgent crops up,' he said to the constable on the desk.

* * *

The inspector walked briskly to the end of King Street and then turned the corner into Sea Road. He enjoyed walking and he loved the sea, so although he could have reached the theatre quicker through the back streets, he chose to go this way. Five minutes later he was on the seafront, near the indoor baths, where he could hear the echoing sound of the bathers below and look through the smoky glass to see the dim shapes of the swimmers splashing about in the water. On chilly days the indoor baths were more popular than the large outdoor bathing pool with its grand diving boards, which was situated at the other end of the two-mile promenade.

He was only going a short distance along, to just beyond the pier, and he walked briskly, savouring the tang of the sea after a morning spent mostly at his desk in the office. The tide was out and the pungency of the seaweed was strong. He inhaled deeply and even lingered by the railings for a few seconds when he reached his destination, enjoying the effect of the sun playing on the sand and highlighting the children in sunhats who were building castles and making sand pies. He allowed his gaze to travel across the expanse of ridged sand to the people larking about further out at the water's edge, before he turned abruptly to look across the road at the still imposing Victoriana theatre.

Could do with a facelift, he thought. This time of day, without lights and crowds, it looked decidedly faded and shabby. At least it was still there — it could so easily have been in ruins after the war, leaving Fairbourne without a theatre, except for the tiny one on the pier where they occasionally put on an old time music hall or variety acts. He crossed the road to the Victoriana, reluctant now to leave the smell of ozone and seaweed, and promised himself he would find more time for a glimpse of the sea in future. It not only cleared your lungs but your whole being. Lifted you up and he needed that at the moment, with Superintendent Salk on the warpath because nothing seemed to be happening with this case.

He paused to study the posters outside the building and smiled to himself. They certainly made the actresses look more glamorous and the actors more suave than he now knew any of them to be, but then that's what acting's about, he thought, as he took the semi-circular steps into the foyer two at a time.

There were more photos adorning the walls here, but these were mostly of scenes from the plays and none of the cast were as prominent as the profiles outside.

Settled in Tim Merry's office, he talked to the stage manager first.

'Did Arnold Brand have private means or was he dependent on his acting for a living, Mr Merry?' he asked.

'I never heard that he had anything except what he earned, Inspector. He never threw his money about — at least not in theatrical circles he didn't. Mixed very little, in fact.'

'He wasn't a popular man so perhaps that explains it. But he lived in a nice house in a good district . . . '

'His wife is, shall we say, more of a star than Arnold was,' Tim Merry said. 'She's never out of work, but I know Arnold did have a number of 'rest periods'.'

All the afternoon John Carding gnawed round the idea in his mind but it wasn't until he had Prince Kingly in front of him that he had a bite and made some headway with his notion of blackmail.

Prince was cross because of his ruined afternoon, which he had been planning to spend with his girlfriend.

'With a show every night and two matinees we don't get a lot of time together,' he complained, 'and I'd like to get off as soon as I can.'

'Of course you would, but when people hold back information it takes twice as long to sift all the evidence.'

The man's face gave him away immediately, and the inspector was quick to follow it up. 'I believe you have something to tell me, Mr Kingly? The sooner you do so the faster you'll be able to go.'

'I know *nothing* about the murder. I've already told you I was in my dressing room having a bite to eat between shows.'

'But perhaps you have other knowledge about Arnold Brand. For instance, did he know your real name or anything else about you?'

Prince Kingly pulled a face. 'I might have known you'd ferret that out. All right, Inspector, you win. Arnold *had* found out my real name and background. He knew I'd been in a bit of trouble with the police when I was a lad. It wasn't much — I'd got in with a gang and after one bad street fight they nicked some of us. It was a long time ago but I didn't want it broadcast so I paid him to keep quiet.'

'How much and how regularly?'

'Ten quid a week. He threatened to tell the newspapers. I didn't want to risk that. I'd

82

have denied it, of course, but some promotion-happy reporter would have checked up. You see I'm just beginning to be someone, Inspector; it's been a long, hard pull but my name's getting known, and at the end of this season I've a chance of a London musical. The timing's wrong for an article saying: 'Prince Kingly, soon to be starring in the West End of London, was once a young tearaway called Joe Smith.' I'm not established enough to ride it yet, and bloody Arnold Brand knew it.'

'How long did you expect to pay for his silence?'

Prince shrugged. 'Who knows? 'Til the end of the season here. If I pull off the musical, well, then I'd probably mention it myself if the climate was right. If you're big enough you can get away with a slightly unsavoury background, though I don't expect I'd have ever told it unless I was pushed. Know what I mean? Can I go now, Inspector?'

'Yes, Mr Kingly.'

Prince turned back when he reached the door. 'I didn't kill him,' he said, 'but between you and me I'm not sorry someone did.'

*　★　*

Roger Johnson was the inspector's next 'victim', and his line of questioning was the same — finding out more about his offstage life.

Roger was as noncommittal as it was possible to be. 'Yes, I did go out with Betty once or twice,' he said, 'but there was nothing serious in it. I take out many different girls from time to time.'

'Among them Nicola Coates, Mr Johnson?'

'She's only a child,' he said, 'but, yes, I've been out with her a couple of times too.'

Inspector Carding made a pretence of consulting his notes. 'You told me you hadn't cared much for Arnold Brand — that he 'thought a deal too much of himself'. As you shared a dressing room with him, I imagine you knew a bit about the type of man he was?'

Roger's face looked for a moment like the long, thin faces one could make in the funfair hall of mirrors, as he replied, 'I'm not sure that I understand what you mean, Inspector. We had very little to do with each other. He didn't like me any more than I liked him.'

'Why was that?'

'No particular reason. At least as far as I know there wasn't.' Roger's shrug shouted disdain. John Carding's eyebrows moved very slightly upwards in a query as he stared back at the actor. As usual it had the desired effect and brought forth a few more words.

'He was coarse and didn't appreciate quality in anything or anybody.'

'But you must have thoughts, even about someone you don't get on with, especially when you are thrown together as you two were.'

'Look, Inspector, Crystal came along whenever she could. Always on matinee days between performances and I cleared out. It suited me, as a matter of fact, because I like walking and I've never been one to hang about in my room when I'm not working. We were in there together long enough to change before and after the show, that's all.'

'Why didn't you like him?'

'I told you — he was vain. Had an unpleasant manner. Ask anyone here and they'll tell you the same.'

'But I'm asking you.'

Roger's face twitched. 'And I've told you.'

'That he had an inflated ego. There must have been more for so much dislike among so many people.'

'He was a womanizer. And he treated his own wife rough.' Roger half rose. 'Is that all, Inspector?'

'For the moment, yes. Thank you, Mr Johnson.' As he reached the door, John Carding said, 'By the way, did you lend Crystal Holman some books?'

It almost always disconcerted people if he asked a question when they thought he had finished. Roger Johnson stopped with his long, lean fingers already on the doorknob.

'Not recently,' he said, 'but I did borrow some from her.'

'Arh, and have you returned those to her?'

'Yes, Inspector, I have.'

'Can you remember when?'

'No, no, I can't. Oh yes, I lent them to Betty, but she's given them back to Crystal now, I think.'

'What books were they?'

'Good heavens, does it matter?' It was obvious from his tone that Roger was getting exasperated.

'It could.'

'One was called *Look Back in Anger*, one was by Graham Greene — I can't remember what it was called — and there was a Kipling there too, I think.'

'Thank you, Mr Johnson.' He knew his studied politeness was having an effect, as it usually did on recalcitrant interviewees.

As Roger left, carefully closing the door quietly behind him, John Carding had the distinct feeling that the actor would have loved to have slammed it hard. He recalled his comment on the murdered man — *thought a deal too much of himself* — and gave a wry smile. 'So do you,' he said softly to the empty room. 'I wonder why?'

★ ★ ★

Betty Morse was in a temper. 'I *am* sorry to have to ask you to come in this afternoon,' John Carding said pleasantly, 'but I'm sure you appreciate the need to clear this up quickly.'

He watched the anger in her eyes and remembered what his sergeant had said about them on that first occasion. A smile bubbled up inside him, but he didn't let it rise to the surface, as he thought that George Binns made a study of eyes as well as handwriting. Especially ladies' eyes!

'I'll come straight to the point, Miss Morse,' he said. 'When you returned the books to Crystal Holman, was she on her way out?'

'I don't know — she may have been.'

'Yet you kept her talking in that room for at least twenty minutes. Why?'

'I didn't keep her talking,' Betty said angrily. 'We . . . just chatted. I didn't even know it *was* twenty minutes — you said that.'

The inspector smiled. 'Wasn't it a strange time to go to her room? I understand that the entire cast knew she used to go to Arnold

Brand's dressing room between the matinee and the evening house.'

'I didn't think about it,' Betty muttered. 'I saw the books there. Roger had borrowed them originally, lent them to me, and I had finished them. I can't think why you're making such an issue over a few books. They can't have anything to do with Arnold Brand's murder.'

The inspector noticed that she usually gave him his full name. 'What were the titles of the books?' he said.

'Titles? I don't remember. Oh, I think there was a Kipling one there. Roger and I are both Kipling fans.'

'And Crystal. Would you say she was a Kipling fan too?'

'How should I know, Inspector? You must ask her — or Roger,' she added. John Carding now allowed a half smile to ripple across his weathered face as he changed the subject.

'I believe you said you got on well with the murdered man,' he said gently.

'Yes. He wasn't popular but I had to work with him. In one of the plays he was my husband. No point in fanning an atmosphere.'

'Very sensible attitude. But underneath you hadn't any more time for him than the others, I suspect.'

She didn't answer.

'He does seem to have been a particularly unlovable character,' he said. 'Blackmail is an ugly word.'

Her eyes really did seem to be burning now, and her voice was sharp. 'Blackmail? Who said anything about blackmail?'

'I did. Was he blackmailing you, Miss Morse?'

'Oh my God.' She covered her face with her hands and sobbed. John Carding looked round uncomfortably. He hated women bursting into tears on him, but he had a job to do, and in spite of his easy manner of questioning, he came down heavily when he thought it necessary and almost always got his information faster than anyone else at the station.

'Perhaps you had better tell me in your own words about it. I'll help all I can. For instance, when did it start and how much were you paying him?'

She struggled to regain some control and still with her head down she answered him haltingly.

'Only began a month ago. I'm . . . giving him ten pounds a week.'

'And what exactly was he blackmailing you about?'

She looked up then and anger showed,

even through the tears still clouding her magnificent eyes.

'You mean you were guessing? You didn't know he was blackmailing me? You pig. You mean, dastardly *pig*.'

John scratched his cheek. 'Now, wait a moment, Miss Morse. I know a great deal more than you might imagine but I need to hear it from you. You see, you weren't the only person Arnold Brand was blackmailing. I don't believe you murdered him but I must have your version of the relationship between you. You see that, don't you?' His voice was persuasive and she nodded dismally.

'It . . . won't go any further, will it, Inspector?'

'Not if you're innocent of the only crime I'm interested in it won't.' He smiled across the table at her. 'But if I don't have *your* version of the story, then it could be a distorted one that I end up with, and that could complicate matters.'

Suddenly she sat upright, her shoulders back, her tummy pulled in. She brushed away the last of her tears with the back of her hand.

'All right, Inspector, but please, please, please don't let it go any further, I beg of you. I couldn't bear her to be hurt.'

'Come on,' he said, briskly now. 'Let's have the story.'

'Four years ago . . . I had a baby. She's called Lillee.'

'Go on,' he said when the pause seemed permanent.

'Well, can't you guess? You did about the blackmail.'

His next remark *was* an inspired guess — one of those that had made Inspector Carding's name respected throughout the Sussex force. 'Tell me about Lillee's father,' he said. He spoke her name with exactly the same intonations that Betty had used.

'He was Chinese, and we were deeply in love. He was killed in a road accident otherwise we would have married. We would have had problems but if we had stayed in England it wouldn't have been so bad eventually. But he died three days before she was born.' Her voice broke. 'I couldn't part with her, and I couldn't get work if she was with me. My mother, God bless her, came to the rescue. She pretended Lillee was an orphan she had adopted. It worked well enough until . . . until this year when . . . when Arnold Brand found out. How, I'll never know.'

'And you paid him,' he paused for a few seconds, watching her closely, 'ten pounds a week for his silence?'

She nodded miserably.

'How long were you prepared to continue doing this, Miss Morse?'

'I — I don't know. I — I did have some vague idea of changing my name at the end of the season and praying I'd never bump into him again.'

'This may sound cruel to you, but in this day and age would it have mattered so much if Arnold Brand had told people that you had a child?'

'Yes, it would.' This time she looked straight at him. 'Roger is very puritanical. He would have finished with me if he had known.'

'Roger Johnson?'

'Yes.'

'I see. That matters to you, does it?'

For a moment she didn't answer, then she looked directly at him and said quietly, 'Yes.'

'Forgive another personal question, please. Are you and Roger planning on marriage?'

'I don't know. No, of course not. I mean, we haven't discussed it but — yes, I hope so,' she said, letting tears run unchecked down her cheeks.

'And what would happen to Lillee then?' The inspector's voice was gentle.

'My mother was prepared to keep her.'

'Thank you, Miss Morse. And don't worry about the truth of Lillee's parentage being leaked. It won't be.'

For a moment he thought she was going to kiss him; the joy and relief on her face was almost more than he could bear. He was tempted not to stop her at the door with his final question, but the policeman in him won.

'What *did* you talk about for over twenty minutes in Crystal Holman's room?' he said.

A stricken look enveloped her features as she turned back to face him.

'About Roger,' she said quietly. 'I heard that Crystal had two dates with him last week.'

'I see. So you really went to warn her off. To tell her to stick to Arnold and leave your boyfriend alone.'

'Not exactly to warn her off; more to check the lay of the land, I suppose. She's a married woman and nothing can come of it for her. You see, I've never wanted anyone since Lillee's father died and — I'm sorry, I'm rambling, Inspector. The truth is I never meant to stay long, just to catch her before she went to Arnold's room, but things became a bit heated.'

'You quarrelled?'

'Yes.' Betty's voice was very quiet now. 'She said it was none of my business and she would see whoever she liked. I wasn't surprised at her but I was at Roger.'

'Why was that?'

'He's very straight, very correct, you know. I think she made all the play for him and he was too courteous to snub her.'

'Thank you, Miss Morse.'

* * *

Inspector Carding was back at the police station by ten minutes to five and Sergeant Binns was already there.

'Fetch a couple of coffees from the machine, will you, George?' he said. 'And a KitKat or something. I had a scrappy lunch.' He fished in his pocket for some loose change. 'Well, the blackmail thing is true, George. Prince Kingly and Betty Morse definitely, and who knows how many others? I think Brand made a good living from it. Modest amounts — he was drawing ten quid a week from those two. Ten fools like that and he had a hundred a week for the rest of the season.'

'Or for life.'

'I think he was clever enough not to follow it up. But if he bumped into them again — anywhere on the theatre circuit — then he simply held out his hand.'

'No wonder someone did for him.'

'Yes, it's a motive, but it multiplies the

number of suspects. Out of a company of six actors and actresses — we won't count the stagehands and electricians for the moment — he was blackmailing at least two of them. What about the other areas of his life? There's probably someone in most towns who cringed when they saw his name on the billboards, knowing he would seek them out with threats of spilling the beans if they didn't pay up.'

'But where did he find so many with skeletons in the cupboard, chief?'

'He was clever, George. Cunning's a better word for it, I think. Nothing earth shattering but he found the Achilles heel of his victims. Went poking for it. With Kingly it was ambition and image — he banked on the man's vanity and it worked. With Betty Morse it went deeper. A child out of wedlock — what's more, a Chinese child, her father killed a few days before the birth. The kid's four now and Betty's pinning her hopes on marrying Roger Johnson, although I wouldn't think it likely from what I've seen and heard.'

'How d'you mean, chief?'

'He dated Crystal Holman twice last week. That's what Betty went to talk to her about; find out what was going on. But there's still something odd about that, you know, George, because according to Betty he's a bit of a purist — it's the reason she fell for the blackmail bit. Reckoned it would ruin her chances with Roger Johnson if Brand told him the truth.'

'So?'

'He wouldn't approve of going with a married woman, not if he really is as narrow minded as Betty thinks. What about you? Any leads?'

George Binns picked up the beaker of coffee. 'Might be. I went to the pub lunchtime, gossiped to some of the regulars. They knew Brand but no-one came up with anything odd. Not the hate we found in the theatre, but a general feeling of dislike. 'Too damn nosy', one old boy said, and 'sniffing out your private business like a damned bloodhound' is how someone else put it. All of which ties in with what you've just been saying, doesn't it, chief?'

'Mmm. Anything else?'

'Iris Brand wasn't there but I talked to the housekeeper. Not fiercely loyal to either of them.' He grinned at the inspector. 'If I ever live in that kind of style I'll make damn sure the people I employ don't talk about me so freely.'

The inspector laughed softly. 'What did you discover?'

'They used to have terrible rows about

Robert Mantle. He's been around a bit longer than six months, by the way. Once he was there at a supper party with several others. He was the last to leave and in the hall he and Brand started slanging each other and it ended in fisticuffs. Apparently he has one hell of a temper and a hefty punch to match it. He finished up with a bruised chin, but Brand had a black eye and a cut lip. This happened during one of his 'resting periods', and according to Mrs Mac he was very subdued for a couple of weeks after that bout.'

'What did Iris do while this was taking place?'

'She came out and begged them to stop, apparently, and Robert shouted at her to keep away. Oh yes, and afterwards, when Arnold had gone off to the bathroom to clean up, he said, 'My God, I'm sorry, Iris, but he had it coming to him. He's been baiting me all evening.' And she replied, 'Never mind, darling, some day this will all be behind us.''

'How long ago?'

'Early spring, she said, before this play started. Another thing she told me was that Arnold used to bring his girlfriends to the house when Iris was away touring.'

'The one clear thing that emerges from all this is the fact that no-one seems to be mourning Arnold Brand overmuch. How about that actress in *Lads and Lassies?* Anything more on her?'

'Name of Gloria Welsh. Was eighteen and pregnant.'

'Was she?' Carding whistled softly. 'And our blackmailer was in that cast. Anything about Gloria Welsh's background?'

'Not yet, but DC Jones is working on it.'

'And the gun?'

'Not been located yet.'

'I have to see Salk tomorrow. He'll want more than we've got at present. You get off now, George, and tomorrow morning one of us will have another chat to Iris's boyfriend Rob.'

8

John Carding studied the handwriting on the notepad he had used for his suspects' names and addresses. Doesn't mean a thing to me, he thought, and according to George it only showed that Nicola Coates was the most naturally truthful of them all. That the others had lied, he didn't doubt — but had they lied about anything important in the catching of Arnold Brand's murderer, or simply to protect themselves from unsavoury publicity?

George always said 'Graphology isn't conclusive but it can lead the way' and the inspector respected his sergeant's knowledge of it. He had said once, 'I only dabble, chief. It's a big subject and takes years to learn properly,' but the inspector knew how thorough his sergeant was, and that his dabbling would be as good as some expertise.

He dealt with a few routine tasks before calling on Betty Morse at her lodgings. He had not been able to get her out of his mind for several hours, and his decision to see her in her home environment was sudden. At first she had seemed to him to be full of confidence, an ambitious and even rather hard actress, but now he found himself hoping she was not involved in Arnold's murder.

He seldom allowed himself to become too interested in anyone he met during the course of his work, but it did happen from time to time. His thoughts now concentrated on her story. He admired the pluck she had shown in keeping the child. It would surely have been possible for her to have made other arrangements for Lillee — an orphanage or institution of some kind perhaps. But she obviously loved her daughter and wanted to give her as normal a life as possible.

You never knew what crosses others had to bear, he thought, as he drove to Betty's part of the town. He liked her independence too, paying for the child's upkeep out of her earnings, which couldn't exactly be in the super tax class. That tenner a week she was giving Arnold for his silence was possibly crippling her more than any of the others he had been extracting money from. Carding was convinced, from what he had learnt of Arnold during this inquiry so far, that the man would not have hesitated in spreading his malicious secrets should anyone default.

It seemed to him that Betty was like a lioness defending her cub. A mother trying to give her child a normal and happy life, and now, replaying in his mind her looks and voice when she spoke about it, he knew there were probably no limits to which she would not go to protect her daughter. What if Arnold had threatened her because she was behind with a payment? She had as much opportunity as anyone in the cast to kill him, and she had a motive, a powerful motive.

He sat in the car for a few moments when he reached the house, working out several scenarios. The most obvious one was that she was giving herself an alibi by spending so long in Crystal's room. If she was Arnold's killer it was a clever move and a daring one also. It would take nerve, but it was a very real possibility. She, more perhaps than anyone else in the theatre, had the most to lose.

Almost reluctantly he opened the door of the car and stepped out into the neat road of Victorian terraced houses. Betty's landlady, a rosy-faced plump little woman, smiled uncertainly at him when she answered the doorbell.

'Miss Morse, yes, I think she's in, sir,' she said in answer to his query. 'Come inside a minute and I'll call her.'

Betty answered his questions with calmness. 'No, I didn't deliberately keep Crystal talking. We both got rather heated and I didn't give a thought to the fact that it was a matinee day and we all knew where she went and what happened then. The books were there, waiting to be returned, and I simply picked them up and went along to her room.'

'If you *had* thought about it, would it have made any difference?'

'Not at that stage, Inspector Carding, because I was pretty worked up. Had I realized before I went I would probably have left it until the next day to return the books.' She gazed at him steadily. 'I was angry and upset and I didn't give the day of the week a single thought. That's the truth, Inspector, I swear it to you.'

'When was the last time you and Roger saw each other offstage, Miss Morse?'

She didn't even have to think about that one. 'A couple of Sundays ago. We weren't exactly on a date, but we were on the same train to London.'

'How did that come about, Miss Morse? If you weren't together, I mean?' His voice was low and quite gentle.

For a moment she hesitated and he thought she wasn't going to answer that particular question, then she said quietly, 'I was already on the train when he ran through the barrier and caught it by the skin of his teeth. The guard had his flag raised when Roger rushed on. I was in the next carriage and after a few moments I — ' She stopped as though she hadn't meant to tell him as much, then with a shrug she said. 'Well, I walked through so we could travel together.'

'This would be the Victoria train?'

'Yes. I was going to see my mum and Lillee.'

'And where was Roger going?'

'Victoria initially, but I don't know what his eventual destination was.'

'Did he not mention where he was going?'

'No.'

'But you talked, I suppose, during the journey?'

Betty looked down towards her feet before answering.

'I think I did most of the talking. He didn't seem to want company and I was sorry I had walked through. I felt most uncomfortable. I've never chased a man before, Inspector, and, well, he simply didn't want to know.'

'And when you reached Victoria?'

'He was in a hurry. He took my arm and helped me down the step and then he asked if I minded if he hurried on because he had an appointment. He strode off along the platform and I lost sight of him very quickly.'

'You never saw him on the return journey?

Didn't co-ordinate times so you could travel back together?'

'No.'

'And I presume you didn't tell him you were going to see your daughter?'

She said firmly, 'I told him I was off to visit my mum.'

'Perhaps he was doing the same? Visiting relatives, I mean?' John Carding suggested, wondering if Roger Johnson had a wife and family he kept quiet about when chatting up the girls. But he kept the thought to himself. Betty was beating herself up enough over the man already, he decided.

'Thank you for your co-operation, Miss Morse.'

As he returned to his car he wondered, was she acting now, or had she been acting yesterday?

Nicola Coates was lodging in the same road and he decided to make his trip worthwhile by surprising her with a visit too.

She seemed nervous to see him, but answered his questions about her movements on the crucial day quietly enough. Just as he was leaving she said, 'Inspector, there is something I noticed. I don't suppose it's important, but . . . ' She stopped and bit her lip.

'Yes, go on,' he encouraged. 'It may not

seem important to you, yet it might be when we put it with other incidents.'

She smiled gratefully at him. 'Well, you know I was looking for Vicky when Crystal screamed?'

He nodded.

'I — I forgot about the cat when — well, you know, with Arnold being murdered — but soon afterwards, before you and the sergeant and all those policemen arrived, Vicky came rushing along the corridor and she was terrified.'

'How do you know — that she was terrified?'

'Her fur was standing on end — I know that sounds silly but it was. Literally poking up all over her little body, even on her tail. She looked so strange and her eyes were wild. I tell you, she was terrified, Inspector.'

'What did you do with her?'

'I couldn't catch her. She rushed by and went into hiding somewhere. Cats do if they're ill or frightened, and she certainly was frightened. She looked, even in those brief seconds as she fled through, completely wild.'

'Thank you for remembering, Miss Coates. Two things more; from which direction did, er, Vicky, appear, and who else was there when the cat tore by?'

'From the stage door end, I *think*. Well, Crystal was there, of course, and Tim — oh, and Charlie.' She paused, obviously trying to be absolutely correct. 'And Roger. Charlie had just let him in, and I think Prince was there too, and Betty, but I'm not sure about those last two — if they were there when Vicky went by, I mean. I think so. You know, suddenly everyone seemed to be there. I went after the cat because she looked petrified, and there wasn't anything anyone could do for Arnold anyway.'

'You are very keen on animals, aren't you, Miss Coates?'

'Yes. I used to work with them all the time — not with the big cats, although I loved them dearly. They were magnificent animals.'

'Big cats sound like a zoo, a circus or on safari.'

'A circus, Inspector, but it was small and didn't pay much and anyway I had always wanted to go on the stage.'

She was more relaxed and forthcoming in her own room than she had been yesterday at the theatre and he quickly took advantage of this to glean more of her background.

'So which animals did you work with?'

'With the horses. I still miss them, but it was time to move on and try to fulfil my childhood dream of being an actress.'

The idea of the frightened cat simmered in his mind on the return journey. Had the animal witnessed the murder? Escaped into the corridor when the killer left Arnold's room, then fled from the scene? Ironic if my only witness turns out to be a dumb animal, he thought. Was the murderer someone from outside the theatre and had the cat shot out of the room and the building with him — or her — in its panic? He dismissed the idea. If that had happened it would not have returned so quickly; it would have holed up somewhere outside.

Perhaps Vicky had wandered into the dressing room just before Crystal and run in terror from the dead body lying there — or maybe her scream had startled it. Whatever the explanation, it wasn't going to help much, except to verify a time; and the time of the murder was the easiest part so far, he thought, for until the curtain descended at twelve minutes past five Arnold Brand was on stage in full view of an audience. At twenty past six he was found dead. One hour and eight minutes to be accounted for, and any one of the cast or theatre personnel could have gone into that dressing room without arousing suspicion. Then again, an outsider could have already been in there waiting to pounce when Arnold returned.

George reported back just before lunch. He and Detective Constable Jones had paid another visit to Robert Mantle, and to Crystal and Tom Holman.

'Nothing from Rob,' he said. 'He admitted to the black eye he'd once given Arnold, and confessed to having a foul temper when roused. 'But murder's not my line,' he said. 'Not with a gun or any weapon. I'll fight a man with my fists but that's all.' Otherwise routine — he has an alibi for the time the murder took place. He was in his dressing room at the theatre in Worthing from the end of the matinee there until the close of the evening performance at ten past ten. A Mr Andrew Clockton was with him all the while between the two houses. I've checked this and it's right. He's an impresario and wants Robert Mantle for his next production. Apparently our Rob is really a song and dance man with a passion for the legit theatre. Andrew Clockton was with him the entire time — they had sandwiches and coffee sent in, and several witnesses from among the cast who popped into his dressing room during the period can vouch for this. Then we went to see the Holmans, and I think that probably Tom Holman is another of Brand's blackmail clients.'

'I thought we might come across a few more,' Carding said dryly. 'What's the skeleton in the cupboard there?'

'This is guesswork, chief, but while we were there — and he was as gruff and uncooperative as before — he had a telephone call from Hearts and Flowers, the romance publishers. Obviously I couldn't hear the whole conversation, but I got the gist. He told them he'd phone them later, but the person at the other end had a penetrating voice and it came through quite clearly. Jones and I both heard it. He said, 'Hullo, Tom — Bill Chesil here. Can you have *Heart's Desire* ready for me to look at when you come up next week?'

'Tom cut in pretty quickly, but I gathered they want to put it in their lists a few months earlier than scheduled. My idea is that Arnold found out that Tom was writing romances for a mostly women's market, and having met the man I'd say it was something he wouldn't want spread around, wouldn't you?'

'Yes. And he paid Brand the usual tenner a week to keep it under his hat. That man had a positive genius for seeking and finding the most vulnerable spot in a person's makeup. And if he *was* drawing hush money from him, it gives Tom Holman a double motive, as it were. Blackmail and Crystal's affair with Arnold.'

The telephone on Inspector Carding's desk rang. 'Carding here. No, don't go for a minute, George,' he said to his sergeant, then turned back to the phone. 'Good.' He wrote something on the pad in front of him. 'Thanks very much.'

'We've got the address of Gloria Welsh's mother, George. I think you and I will take a trip to town and see her. What else have we on the books that's urgent?'

'Your audience with Superintendent Salk, sir.'

'Oh Lord, I'd forgotten that. We'll go immediately afterwards.'

★ ★ ★

The two detectives drove to London the following morning. Sergeant Binns knew better than to ask how the meeting with the super went, but John Carding enlightened him anyway.

'We have a stay of execution, George,' he said, bringing a twinkle to the sergeant's eyes yet again with his choice of words. 'Superintendent Salk is going to be on a course for ten days and I assured him that of course the case will be brought to a satisfactory conclusion by the time of his return.'

Mrs Welsh lived near Paddington station, in a first-floor flat in what must once have been an elegant house. Now it looked rather shabby, the paint flaking from the windowsills and front door. There were four bells and, selecting 'I. Welsh', the inspector rang and waited.

The woman who opened the door a fraction and peered out was small and grey haired.

'Mrs Welsh?' the inspector queried.

'Yes.'

He showed his card. 'May we have a word with you, please? We think you could assist us in one of our enquiries. Detective Inspector Carding and Sergeant Binns.'

'Well, you had better come in, I suppose.' She opened the door wider.

'Thank you, Mrs Welsh. It won't take long.'

They followed her upstairs into a small kitchen. 'I've got the decorators in the living room,' she explained, 'so it'll have to be in here if you don't mind.'

'Not at all. I'll come straight to the point. Your late daughter was an actress, I believe, Mrs Welsh?'

She looked startled. 'Yes, that's right,' she said.

'And when she died, five years ago, she was

touring in a play called *Lads and Lassies*. Is that correct?'

'Yes, but I don't see — after all this time how . . . ' She broke off and her eyes filled with tears.

The inspector said gently, 'Would you still have a programme of that play, Mrs Welsh? What we want, you see, are the names of everyone who was in it.'

'I haven't any programmes,' she said. 'This is a small flat and I haven't room for too much. Anyway, Gloria only had a small part.'

'Can you recall anyone else in the play, Mrs Welsh?'

She drew her lips tightly together and shook her head.

'Does the name of Arnold Brand ring any bells?'

'Yes, he was in it,' she said.

'Did you ever meet him?'

'No.'

'But you knew he was in that play?'

'I'd probably recognize the other names in it too if you said them. I've always had a good memory. Why, is it important?'

The murder in Fairbourne had not made the headlines in the national press — it had, in fact, only merited a paragraph — and possibly Mrs Welsh didn't take a daily paper regularly.

'Arnold Brand died the other day, Mrs Welsh. I am trying to tie up some loose ends.'

'Not a natural death then if they send the police to investigate,' she said.

'He was murdered. That's why we are tracing people who knew him.'

'I can't see how my Gloria once being in a play with him can help. She's been gone five years now.'

'Did she ever mention him?'

'I don't think so. Maybe in a list of actors and actresses she was working with. Hers was more or less a walk-on part, you see. Her career was only just beginning.' Her tone changed to one of pride. 'But she would have gone on from there if she'd lived. She was talented, was my Gloria, as well as being beautiful to look at.'

'I'm sorry to have had to bother you with all this,' Carding said quietly. 'It's just routine, Mrs Welsh.' He stood up. 'We'll let ourselves out, save you coming down. Thank you for seeing us.'

When they were once more in the car, Sergeant Binns said, 'Not much there, chief.'

'I didn't really expect there to be, George. But the girl committed suicide, she was pregnant, and Arnold Brand was in that play. He could have been blackmailing her — if he knew about the pregnancy he undoubtedly

113

would have been. It was a long shot but something might have fitted.' He turned to face his sergeant. 'Leave no stone unturned is a good motto, and frankly, with so many who wished him dead, although so far none of the motives seem strong enough, I'm puzzled.'

'You think it is an inside job, chief?'

'Well, Charlie swears he never left his post and no-one unauthorized went past him. And present in the theatre that afternoon were the cast, minus Strong the ASM and understudy. Tim Merry the stage manager, Harry the odd-job man and Doris the wardrobe mistress were all there. Out of that lot the only ones who left the theatre were Roger Johnson, who had a cup of coffee and a couple of teacakes in the cafe opposite — the waitress remembers serving him and confirms that he was there about forty minutes, and that ties in with the time he returned and Charlie let him in — and Doris, the wardrobe mistress, who went to the shop round the corner and was gone about half an hour. No witnesses except Charlie, who saw her go out and return with a shopping bag and that was just before Crystal discovered Brand's body. Arnold didn't leave the stage until twelve minutes past five when the curtain came down on the matinee, and Crystal Holman found him at twenty past six when she went to his dressing room for a bit of slap and tickle. If anyone in that audience had stayed behind to kill him, when and how did they leave the theatre? The only opportunity that I can see would be when Charlie rushed along the corridor in answer to Crystal's scream. The first thing he did after he had established that Arnold was in fact dead was to lock the panic bolts on the stage door, and check that no-one was hiding anywhere in the theatre itself.'

He pulled out a packet of cigarettes and offered one to his sergeant, who was in the driving seat.

'Now we're up here let's go and see Bill Chesil, the Hearts and Flowers man, George. D'you know where Netley Street is?'

Sergeant Binns took a map from the compartment in front. 'Can soon find out, chief — I put the London street map in before we set out this morning.'

Carding smiled satisfactorily.

★ ★ ★

There was nothing ornate about the building. A simple brass plate outside announced *Hearts and Flowers (Publishers) Established 1920.*

'Very ordinary,' Sergeant Binns commented.

'What did you expect, George? Cupid in lights over the door?'

George grinned. 'Dunno, really. But my missus reads these books and goes all moony eyed over 'em. I asked her once what the appeal was. Know what she said? 'Well, it's nice to pretend you're the girl all these exotic things happen to. Sometimes when I'm reading I think I'm that girl with the lovely figure and the peaches and cream complexion.' Strange fancies women have, I reckon. There's nothing wrong with her complexion. She's short and plump and . . . well, homely, if you know what I mean, but I wouldn't want her any other way. Still, she enjoys her dreams so they do no harm, I suppose.'

They had driven into the car park at the side of the building and Inspector Carding laughed. 'Escapism, George. But it's hard to imagine Tom Holman writing that sort of book.'

★   ★   ★

Bill Chesil was engaged so they sat down to wait. He emerged after ten minutes or so, with a matronly woman dressed in blue. After escorting her to the lift, he walked along the crimson-carpeted corridor and extended his hand to them.

116

'Sorry to keep you, gentlemen. Will you come into the office?' They followed him. 'How can I be of assistance?' he asked when they were introduced and seated.

'You can tell us if Tom Holman writes for you, Mr Chesil.'

'Ah.' He smiled across his desk at them both. 'I do make it a rule never to disclose pseudonyms,' he said.

'Of course. But the police do not ask out of idle curiosity, as you know.'

'Why don't you ask — ' he hesitated slightly as if to prove he wasn't familiar with the name, ' — Mr Holman himself?'

'We probably will but I doubt he will tell us. A reticent man, is Mr Holman. I cannot, of course, force you to disclose private information at this stage, but I had hoped you would.'

'If I may ask you one thing, Inspector. What has this . . . this Mr Holman done?'

'A fair question, Mr Chesil. As far as we know, nothing. But his name has cropped up in an investigation we are conducting and it is important that we know as much as possible. If he writes for Hearts and Flowers, as we are fairly sure he does, it would help us to have confirmation and to know the name he writes under. Our source of information would not of course be disclosed, Mr Chesil.'

The editor drummed his fingers on his desk for a moment, and then he looked straight at the inspector.

'Are you a married man, sir?' he said.

'Yes, Mr Chesil, I am.'

'Your wife may enjoy our books, Inspector. I hope she does. So many women do; it takes them out of themselves and into another, sometimes more dreamlike world. A place where nice things happen to them, a romantic, wonderful world. We deal in escapism, Inspector, and perhaps your wife sometimes reads some of our top authors' books, such as the lady who was here just before you — Jayne Matthews. Or Priscilla Chester maybe, another of our prolific and well-read writers. If so, I do hope she enjoys them.'

The inspector rose. 'Thank you, Mr Chesil. You have been most courteous, and I hope we shall not have to trouble you further. I will recommend Priscilla Chester to my wife for future reading.'

The editor walked to the lift with the two policemen.

'Blimey,' Sergeant Binns said when they were once more in the car park. 'Priscilla Chester — Tom Holman. I don't believe it!'

118

9

It was the middle of the following morning
when the desk sergeant answered the
telephone to hear a Scottish voice say, 'Tell
Inspector Carding to look in Crystal's room
for the gun.'

'Who is this speaking?' he asked, but the
line went dead. He alerted John Carding
immediately and the inspector was at the
theatre ten minutes later. It was closed.

He telephoned Tim Merry at his house.

'There's no matinee today, Inspector, and
the cleaners are usually finished by ten, so
Harry, who keeps a key, is always away by five
past. The box office doesn't open until six
— they sell the advance tickets in the
information bureau, and in the caravan on
the seafront, you see,' he explained, 'but if it's
important I'll come down now.'

'No, leave it until later. What time do the
cast arrive?'

'Usually between 6.30 and seven. It's
curtain up at 7.30. I'm there by six most
evenings, though.'

'And no-one can get in before you?'

'That's right. Well, only Harry, the

billboard man, you know, but there's no cause for him to go in again.'

Inspector Carding decided to give whoever had telephoned a shock by not rushing to the Victoriana. Whoever it was would be on tenterhooks all day — it was probably a bogus call anyway — but now he knew the only two people who could get inside the theatre were Tim Merry and Harry, the odd-job man, he would make the telephone caller sweat.

'I'll come and see you just after six tonight, Tim.' He pulled a sheaf of notes towards him and when Sergeant Binns came in with a cup of coffee for him he said, 'Bring yours in, too, George, and we'll pool our brains.'

George did as he was asked.

'Pity we can't trace that call,' Carding said when they had settled. 'Still, we can check if any of the suspects were out this morning. Get DC Jones on to it, will you? Someone might have seen whoever it was, but I doubt it. He'd make sure no landlady or neighbour saw him going into a phone box, or even leaving the house.'

'And as they're all actors, it could have been any of them, chief.'

The inspector wrote on his pad; Roger Johnson — Prince Kingly — Robert Mantle — Tim Merry — Charlie Ferguson — Tom Holman.

'You think it *was* one of them, chief?' Sergeant Binns drank his coffee noisily.

'It's likely. Then again it could be another of Arnold's victims whom we haven't caught up with yet.' He picked up his biro again and added Peter Strong — understudy and assistant stage manager — to his list. 'All we do know is that it was a man either with or putting on a Scottish accent. Then there's the odd-job man himself. He would have the best opportunity. His background has been checked and nothing's come up that suggests any sort of connection with the victim.'

'He was the first one to express a strong dislike for Arnold Brand, chief. Although he didn't know he was dead then.'

'We are assuming he didn't know, George. He might be as good an actor as anyone treading the boards of that stage now. He is also a key holder.'

* * *

Crystal and Tom Holman sat opposite each other at the breakfast table, not speaking. She wondered how she could have married such a stick-in-the-mud. He had seemed so glamorous when they met; now his rugged features looked coarse, his hair was thinning, and as for sex . . . I suppose he finds it in those

121

sloppy books he writes, she thought. She sighed and buttered another piece of toast. If only this murder business was all cleared up. That stupid inspector — another stick-in-the-mud. Goodness, she could twist him round her little finger. The first hint of tears, the slightest tremble in her voice and he was all softness and concern. It was frightening, though, to think that someone had got in and murdered Arnold. And if Betty hadn't returned those books and got herself all steamed up about Roger, she might have been in with Arnold when his killer struck. She shivered and said, 'Who do you think murdered Arnold, Tom?'

She knew he had heard her because his ears twitched slightly, but he went on reading his post and eating his breakfast.

'Tom, for God's sake, listen to me! I'm worried.'

He put the letter down. 'Why? You've already told me it wasn't you, and frankly, Crystal, I'm not surprised. You'd never shoot straight enough. Or are you afraid the killer will return and do for you too?'

'Don't,' she whimpered. 'It's frightening enough as it is. It couldn't have been one of the cast, surely? I mean, we know them all — it has to be someone outside, doesn't it, Tom?'

'Probably a jealous wife he never told you about.'

'My God, Tom, how often do I ask you for comfort, for anything, and when I do need it desperately you — '

Tom Holman looked across at her. 'Save the histrionics for the stage, Crystal. And why should I offer you comfort, or anything else for that matter? You've two-timed me almost all of our married life — Arnold Brand and how many others?'

'Tom . . . '

But he had returned to his breakfast and his post.

* * *

Prince Kingly went into the town centre to buy a pie from the small shop near Oliver's Memorial. 'They're the best in town,' he said to the shopkeeper, who had the figure of a man who endorsed his own products. He saw Peter Strong waiting by the telephone box on the corner and waved to him, but the actor didn't acknowledge him and seemed to be scanning the road from the opposite direction. Wonder who he's waiting for? Prince thought. He shrugged and went off towards the seafront. He had hired a beach hut as soon as he knew he would be spending the summer season in Fairbourne. It was small but adequate, and when Cheryl, his girlfriend of the moment, was free it became a cosy love nest. Today he was alone because she was working away for two nights, demonstrating her firm's makeup in the big stores further along the coast. He put his pie on the small table for later and changed into scarlet trunks. Flexing his muscles, he breathed deeply several times to pull in his stomach and make himself feel taller. Then he stepped outside and spread a towel on the stones for himself.

Later he would go for a swim, but first he liked to assess the talent. After a while he relaxed and picked up his book. It was an American crime novel but lying there in the sun his mind wandered to the real-life murder that had taken place at the Victoriana last week. He was now ten quid a week better off and if that inspector kept his word no-one need know that Prince Kingly was originally orphaned Joe Smith from Hackney, or that he'd once been in trouble with them himself.

Prince Kingly, the future musical comedy king, would have a more exotic background than that. Nothing too fancy but with enough romance and mystery to appeal to the sort of fans he hoped to attract. His mind swivelled with his eyes as a suntanned blonde in an emerald bathing suit walked by. 'What a sight for sore eyes,' he murmured, sexual desire stimulating his body yet again.

★ ★ ★

Roger Johnson met Nicola when he went to Sainsbury's that morning. His mother always dealt with Sainsbury's. 'Everything is so clean and fresh,' she had told him when he first started out on his own. 'Good quality, Roger, always go for that.'

He went in for some of their cheese. He enjoyed a lump of cheese with a banana at lunchtime when there was no matinee. He saw Nicola coming towards him and knew he wouldn't be able to avoid stopping. It was a long, wide shop and there were several prams parked down the centre on the black and white tiled floor, so there was no escape route. He felt embarrassed about Nicola because in the early days of the season he had taken her out a few times in between dating Betty. Nicola was a nice girl. The sort of girl his mother would approve of. A bit like his sister really — perhaps that was what had attracted him to her in the beginning. But the romance soon palled for him, although he knew it hadn't for her. He found Betty far more interesting, but he still kept his distance from them both. He had no intention of getting himself tied up with any woman for years yet.

As they drew level with each other, he looked down at the shopping bag in her hand and said, 'You beat me to it today, Nicola.'

She smiled at him with her lips and her eyes and he felt rather ashamed of his thoughts. Nicola said, 'I would have got your stuff too if you'd said what you wanted, Roger. But it's not too crowded at the moment.'

'That's good. I want to have time for a swim later.' He made to move on but she said, 'So do I. It's such a lovely day. Whereabouts do you go? Oh dear, that sounds as though I'm prying — '

'Not at all,' he cut in quickly. 'As a matter of fact I'm glad I bumped into you like this because I don't much fancy swimming alone. How would it be if I meet you in an hour's time and we go together?' He felt embarrassed at the pleasure he had brought to her face because he knew how false he was being.

'Why, Roger, that would be lovely,' she said.

'I'll see you by the entrance to the pier in an hour then,' he said, smiling as he moved away.

★ ★ ★

Robert Mantle telephoned Iris just after eight o'clock that morning. 'It's a beautiful day,' he said. 'How about a spin somewhere?'

'Do you think we ought to, Rob?' she asked.

'Why ever not, sweetheart? If the police are keeping their eye on us, as they well may be, what harm can a day out together do? They know about us, and we know that we are not guilty of murder. Besides, I think it will do you good to get out of the house for a bit, my love. Apart from the theatre each night, you've hardly stirred.'

'I'm so tired, Rob. Absolutely exhausted.'

'I know.' His voice was gentle. 'We won't do anything energetic, and you need do nothing but sit in the car and be driven somewhere quiet and peaceful. I'll bring a picnic so you won't even have to mix with anyone else in a restaurant or pub — just the two of us, darling. And I'll get you home by four this afternoon so you'll have plenty of time to rest before your performance.'

'All right Rob. It — it does sound tempting.'

'Bless you, darling. I'll be with you about ten. And Iris?'

'Yes, Rob?'

'I love you. I always will.'

'Darling,' she said on a sob, 'I love you too.'

Tim Merry sat in his garden reading the script of a comedy a little-known writer had sent him. It wasn't making him laugh, but perhaps it wasn't fair to judge in his present mood.

Although Arnold Brand's murder was still pulling the crowds into the play at the Victoriana, it was a worrying time for Tim. He had had bad vibes about this play — or was it about this company — from the start. Was it because Arnold Brand was in it?

He had not wanted to use the actor but at that eleventh hour there was not much choice. None at all really, and he was a good jobbing actor as well as being an overbearing, egoistic person. After all, it was simply bad luck that the girl in that other play had committed suicide and cast such a blight over the theatre during the run. What *was* that play called, and who else was in it?

His wife came out to join him, bearing a tray with two tall glasses of iced orange.

'Don't look so worried, dear,' she said. 'The police will find whoever did it soon, I'm sure, then you'll be able to get back to normal.'

'Suppose it was one of them?' he said.

'Whoever it was, once the police nail him,

it will clear the air,' she said. 'You worry too much, Tim, and it's not good for you.'

'It gives the theatre a bad name,' he said, 'and of course it's upsetting to think there is a murderer in our midst.'

His wife looked startled. 'You really think it is one of them, don't you, Tim, and not an old enemy of Arnold Brand's who sneaked in and killed him then left Fairbourne for ever?'

He ran a hand distractedly through his thinning grey hair. 'I no longer know what to think, my dear. At first I — I thought like you, but now I don't know.'

'Why, Tim?' Her voice was urgent. 'Is it anything strange that you've noticed? Anything odd someone has done or said?'

He looked up, then started to rise from his chair. 'Telephone, I think,' he said without answering her question.

'Sit still, dear, I'll get it.' She took the empty tray and returned to the house, but was back a few seconds later. 'It's for you, dear. Inspector Carding.'

*   *   *

Charlie Ferguson lived in a neat cottage the other end of the town from the theatre.

'It's a glorious day,' he said to his wife that morning over breakfast. 'I think I'll do a bit of weeding then relax and enjoy the garden for an hour. I've a new book from the library I'm looking forward to reading.'

'Another murder mystery, I'll be bound,' Jean Ferguson said, smiling at him.

'Right first go. D'you need any shopping first, though? I can get it for you when I go for my tobacco, if you like.'

'No, dear. I think I'll rush through the housework then join you in the garden today. I've got a new book too — the latest Priscilla Chester romance.'

Twenty minutes later Charlie walked down the road to the newsagents for his tobacco. And as he walked he turned over in his mind the possibilities of who Arnold Brand's murderer was.

If it was an outsider, he thought, then he — or she — could have hidden somewhere in the theatre and come into the dressing room area through the pass door after the performance. But the only chance anyone could have got out was to be hiding in another dressing room or in the backstage loos between the time Arnold was killed and the time he was found because that was the only time when he wasn't in his cubbyhole and the stage door was still open. After that he had the panic bolts in place and pulled them back himself to let Roger in. But if the killer had waited until Charlie had gone into the room when Crystal screamed, he or she would have had several minutes to escape into the street and be away.

If, on the other hand, it *was* a member of the company, the coming and going from Arnold's room would be very much harder to detect.

★ ★ ★

Inspector Carding and Sergeant Binns were at the theatre at ten minutes to six that evening. Tim Merry was already there.

'I came nice and early as you were coming in,' he said nervously.

'Thanks. I would like to see Crystal Holman as soon as she arrives,' John Carding told him.

Tim looked startled. 'Crystal?' he said in a thin voice.

'Yes, but I don't want her to have warning of it. I'd like you to be with me when she comes in and we can all go to her dressing room together. Could we wait in Charlie's little domain, do you think?'

'Why, yes, surely. All of us, Inspector?' Tim's thin face looked more wrinkled and worried than ever.

'No. I'd like to leave Sergeant Binns

131

outside Miss Holman's dressing room — on guard as it were.'

★ ★ ★

Crystal and Roger were the first to arrive. They walked in together.

'Crystal,' Charlie said, as he had been instructed, 'could you hang on a second? Someone wants to see you.'

She went very pale, and seemed relieved when Inspector Carding appeared behind Charlie.

'Sorry to startle you,' he said. 'Could I have a quick word with you in your dressing room, Miss Holman?'

Recovering her composure she said coldly, 'And if I say no, I expect you will enforce the law, Inspector, in spite of your sweet talk.' At her reply, Roger allowed half a smile to play around his lips before walking on.

'Certainly I will,' Carding said softly. 'I won't keep you longer than is absolutely necessary, though. Just a couple of questions.'

She gave an exaggerated sigh. 'It's all very melodramatic, Inspector, but if you must then I suppose you must.'

He and Tim Merry followed her to the dressing room, where Sergeant Binns was standing self-consciously outside.

'No visitors, George?'

'None, sir.'

Inside the room the inspector said quietly, 'I had a telephone call this morning to say that if we searched your dressing room, Miss Holman, we would find the gun that killed Arnold Brand. Have you any idea where we may begin looking?'

It was difficult to know who looked more shocked and surprised, Crystal or Tim Merry. But it was Crystal who recovered first.

'But Inspector Carding,' she said, '*I* didn't kill Arnold so how could you find the gun here?'

'Oh, we may find the weapon, Miss Holman, but that in itself won't prove that you killed him. Only that whoever did is trying to implicate you. Unless of course it still has your fingerprints on. You looked very frightened when Charlie told you someone was waiting to see you just now. Who did you think it was, Miss Holman?'

She put her hands to her lips. 'I didn't know,' she said, 'but I thought — well, I thought it might — might be the m-murderer.'

'And why did you think that?'

'Well, wouldn't you, if you were as close to Arnold as I was?' she retorted, suddenly losing her little-lost-woman image. 'Whoever killed him may have thought I'd seen something. After all I was — was often in his room.'

'*Did* you see anything, Miss Holman?' The inspector's voice was soft again.

'No, Inspector.'

'Well, this shouldn't take long. It's a small enough room to search,' he said with an attempt at levity. He opened the door and beckoned his sergeant in. 'You take that side and I'll take this,' he said.

Tim Merry stood awkwardly by the dressing table and Crystal sat down and watched through the mirror. Both men searched diligently for a few moments, exploring corners, behind the mirror and under the cushions. The watchers were just beginning to look relieved when John Carding picked up the teddy bear which sat on the basket chair in the corner. He prodded it gently, then turned it over and slowly unzipped the back.

When the inspector found the gun inside the soft teddy bear jewel case, Crystal began to tremble and went so white that for a moment John Carding thought she was going to faint. Instead she said shakily, 'How — did — it — get — there?'

'That's what we shall find out, Miss Holman.'

He lifted the weapon out, using a white

134

cloth he had with him for that purpose, and she swung round to face him. 'I didn't do it, Inspector. I didn't kill Arnold — I swear to you. And that — that gun hasn't been here since that night. It couldn't have been — could it?' she whispered.

'Don't fret about that,' he told her. 'Leave it to us. And I would appreciate it if neither of you mentioned the finding of the gun to anyone. That could hamper our enquiries and might be dangerous.' He looked at them both as he said, 'I'm deadly serious now.' He saw the flicker that rippled across George Binns' face as he went on, 'Come, Mr Merry, you must have a great deal to do before curtain up.'

'Yes, Inspector.' As they moved into the corridor he said, 'I'll be so glad when this business is cleared up. Do you think that maybe someone who was in the audience that night . . . or . . . ' he broke off.

'I don't think Miss Holman killed Arnold Brand, if that is any consolation to you,' Inspector Carding said.

They bade good night to Charlie as they left, just as Nicola and Prince came in. George Binns was just starting the car when John Carding said softly, 'That gun I so carefully wrapped up is not the one that killed Arnold Brand, George. The gun in the teddy bear is not a Luger. In fact, from the weight of it I would say it was probably a stage prop. A realistic stage prop, but not the murder weapon. Someone is trying to alter the course of justice and frighten Crystal at the same time. She may not realize she saw something but the killer obviously thinks she did, wouldn't you say?'

George whistled softly. 'Looks like it, chief. I suppose he, or she,' he added quickly, 'hasn't had a chance to get rid of the weapon yet — the real one, I mean. Otherwise why should he play games like this?'

'We shall need to search the entire cast's digs and homes, George, and possibly the stagehands' too. Not sure if we have enough manpower to do that at present. But I think we can eliminate Crystal from our suspects. For the time being anyway,' he added cautiously.

10

'For crying out loud, Crystal, put some pep into it! Half the audience were falling asleep this afternoon, and you fluffed your lines twice,' Tim grumbled after the Wednesday matinee.

'I'm tired,' she said. 'I've been through so much these last few weeks and I'm not sleeping properly with this murder business hanging over us.'

'You aren't the only one. It's affecting us all but you're supposed to be a professional so let's see some proper acting on stage as well as off.'

Her lips quivered and she looked at him like a little girl who has been unfairly told off.

'And don't turn on the waterworks; save that for your performance tonight.' Head down, he walked away, not even seeing Prince and Roger, who were heading for their dressing rooms.

'He looks on the verge of collapse himself,' Prince said. 'He's the most nervy person I've ever met. Even before Arnold's death he was jittery, but I've not seen him in this sort of domineering mood before.'

'He's a perfectionist,' Roger replied. 'At least where his job is concerned, and Crystal gave a pretty poor show by anyone's standards this afternoon. I think he's justified in having a go at her. She'll need to pull her socks up if she doesn't want Doris taking over her role in this play.'

Crystal was thinking along the same lines as she sat facing her image in the mirror above the cluttered shelf filled with her stage makeup. A tiny fluffy white rabbit was there amongst it all, its twin in the mirror reflecting the glittering silver star attached to its ear. In reality it was the maker's trademark but she chose to think that Arnold had bought it for her because he knew she would one day be a star. 'What you hope to be,' he had said when he thrust it into her hands only a few weeks ago. Now, in a rare moment of facing the truth, she recalled her disappointment at the lack of conviction in his voice and her spirited reply, 'What I *will* be, Arnold, you'll see.'

She sat for a few moments, gazing at herself in the centre of the worn mirror. The edges had mostly lost their silver and there was a crack in the top right-hand corner. She had tried to cover this with a glossy picture of herself but the photo wouldn't stick for long and the last time it fell she wearily picked it up and put it in her bag. Now she faced the fact that if she didn't get herself motivated and rivet the audience at this evening's performance, Tim just might put Doris on tomorrow. Crystal was always polite and surface friendly to the understudy, but she was wary of her. Dammit, the woman was good, and Tim was in an unpredictable mood just now. He's so timid and nervy over most things but a martinet when he gets you on stage and he won't let go until everything is right, she thought.

She stood up and shook herself as though trying to free such negative thoughts from her mind. Matinee days were the worst time for her because of what used to happen in the hours between shows. Since Arnold's death she hadn't felt able to stay in the theatre then, and either went to the nearby cafe and spun out a drink and a bun, or else she went home for an hour.

Today she didn't want to go back to the house because Tom would be there and he offered no support at all. True, he didn't know about the gun being found in her teddy bear jewel case, but it was bugging her more and more as time passed and there had been no solution. There was a murderer at large and someone had tried to implicate her. Would they be coming back for her later? Was the act of planting the gun in her room meant to unnerve her? If it was it had definitely achieved that, she thought. Each day she found herself looking over her shoulder, fraught with fear.

Whoever it was may not risk another killing in the theatre, but in her home, in the street; they could pounce any time and anywhere. These thoughts had been haunting her ever since the discovery of the murder weapon and she knew they were taking their toll on her work. Sometimes she wished the inspector had taken her into custody for her own protection. Instead he had told her not to worry about the 'evidence' but under no circumstances to tell anyone. And Tim Merry wondered why she was jittery and not concentrating! He of all people should understand, she thought, as she changed into a blouse and skirt, slipped a cardigan round her shoulders and left the Victoriana to go for a walk along the front. After all, he was the only other person who knew about the gun, apart from the police. Even Charlie at the stage door, who was known by them all as the eyes and ears of the world, didn't know what the inspector had wanted to see her about.

She often saw Roger on the days she went to the cafe and always made a point of sitting at his table. They usually talked about the current play — she flirted with him and had the distinct feeling he enjoyed that, but he was a slow mover where women were concerned, she thought, and anyway he wasn't her type. She just couldn't help fluttering her eyelashes at any man who was reasonably presentable, even if she had no intention of taking it further. It gave her a boost when they responded. Could one of them have planted the gun in her room because she had rejected him in favour of Arnold? If so, which one? Roger, who after all had been pushed from his own dressing room to leave the coast clear for her? Or Prince, who obviously thought he was God's gift to women? Certainly not neurotic Timmy — she remembered calling him that once and he hadn't liked it a bit. Charlie? Hardly because he seemed to take everything in his stride. He simply laughed when she practised her wiles on him as she came and went through the stage door. And until Arnold's murder she had not had much to do with Peter, the understudy. He always disappeared quickly after the show, and now they were too busy getting it right at rehearsal and on stage for any extra flirtatious behaviour.

She reached the promenade and sat on the nearest seat to watch the people walking by. Some sauntering, some hurrying, and in such a wonderful mixture of dress. Crystal loved clothes and enjoyed the panorama of New Look styles, some very obviously created by adding a deep frill or an extra length to the bottom of existing frocks, and some the elegant new Dior look. There were the shorter dresses too and blouses and skirts, shorts and even people in bathing costumes who had come straight from the beach.

Yet today even this colourful parade couldn't prevent her mind from going over and over what had happened and wondering yet again if the person who had shot poor Arnold was a member of the company or someone from another area of the actor's life. In spite of the heat, she shivered at the idea that it was one of them, but who? And why? A jealous wife? But he had told her his wife was cold and unfeeling and that they led separate lives, albeit in the same house. That she had her peccadilloes too. No, somehow she couldn't believe it was Iris Masters who had shot him. Charlie would have known if she had been near the theatre that day.

Almost against her will, Crystal confronted the fact that it was possibly one of the company. Betty, Nicola, even Doris, but what motive did they have? None of them were after Arnold, as far as she knew, but how could you be sure? As she rose to make her way back to the Victoriana, images of the women in the company crowded into her head. Arnold had preferred her to any of them and maybe jealousy was the reason for planting the gun where they did. They all knew she had a soft jewel case in the shape of a teddy bear, whereas not all the men did. Perhaps she should mention this to the inspector. He was one she hadn't got anywhere with, in spite of his sometimes soft manner. For the first time in her life, Crystal wondered if some men could resist her after all. At first she thought he had succumbed as most men did, but now she realized he was just stringing her along to get any evidence out of her.

It wasn't until she was in her dressing room and changing for her first entrance that she had the terrifying thought that her own husband, although he professed not to care, might have seen off this particular rival himself. After all, Tom was a top shot and knew about the teddy jewel case because he had given it to her all those years ago when they first married and he really had been besotted with her. She breathed a sigh of relief that she had had second thoughts and not told him about the gun being found after all. Best to let him think it was still missing. He would only torment her about it.

She perched the little red hat she wore in

the first scene jauntily on her head, tilting it first this way, then that, to get the best angle, pulled the half veil seductively down over her eyes, picked up the shiny red handbag and made her way to the wings. Tonight she'd show them all, especially timorous and angry Tim.

11

'Who's going to watch the climb this afternoon?' Prince said as the rehearsal for the next week's show finished. 'I reckon we could all do with a bit of fun. You gonna come, Crystal?'

She shook her head. 'I'm not in the mood for fun, and I'm surprised any of you are with this — this murder hanging over us all.'

'The police don't seriously think it was one of us who murdered poor Arnold,' Betty said.

'You could have fooled me.' Nicola's voice was sharper than usual. 'That Inspector Carding has had me back and forth like a yo-yo, always asking the same questions but phrased differently, if you see what I mean. It makes you nervous when someone keeps on like that even though you know you had nothing to do with it.'

'It's not just you, Nicola. He's doing it to us all, and let's be fair, he and his team have to, don't they? That's what they're there for, after all, to catch criminals and murderers.' It was Roger Johnson who spoke as he gazed around the assembled group.

'Don't,' Crystal said in a voice only just

above a whisper. 'I can't bear to hear you all talking like this when Arnold — ' She almost swallowed the last part of his name — 'when he . . . he is no longer with us.' She had had second thoughts about whether to tell Tom about the gun being found in her room. She badly wanted to share this knowledge and she was sure that her husband wasn't a murderer.

Better not, she thought, in case Tom took it into his head to come round and 'sort it out'. In certain moods he was quite capable of suggesting this, she knew. And he wouldn't be doing it for her but for the publicity of the gesture.

Crystal could cope when she was on stage at night easier than she could during the daytime when the murder was uppermost in her thoughts. The first night back afterwards had been the worst and she had found it hard not to cry during that performance. To have Peter, the understudy, holding and kissing her instead of Arnold, especially during the final scene, was almost unbearable, but she knew if she let go and broke down Tim Merry would put the understudy on for a few nights, and Doris was good. She was also ambitious and had been overheard to say that she didn't intend to be a dresser all her life, that one day she would be out there centre stage. Crystal did not intend to take any chances.

It was Charlie at the stage door who had told them about the celebrations which took place every year in honour of Edgar Oliver, whom the clock tower in the centre of the town commemorated.

It stood on an island and was unusual in that each of its four faces represented a different aspect of nature. The one facing north was surrounded by paintings of seabirds, the southern one by wild flowers, the eastern-facing clock face showed tiny wild creatures like water voles and stoats, while on the west side were various species of fish. The island itself was kept looking attractive with whatever flowers were in season, and the whole edifice was a credit to the town and to the man who inspired it.

According to Charlie, Edgar Oliver had arrived in Fairbourne in 1836 as a poor young man who, by dint of hard work and a great personality, made good, became mayor and gave back all he had and more to the place which gave him his first chance to make something of himself. Often referred to by the natives as Oliver's Memorial, the column stood sixty-five feet high, while the design round the four faces of the clock was chosen to reflect Edgar Oliver's own passionate interests as well as various aspects of the seaside town.

The day began early at the fish-market where there were lectures and demonstrations about the fish to be found in the sea at Fairbourne. The afternoon concentrated on nature walks across the cliffs with a guide to point out the many wild flowers which grew both on the clifftop and in the glens and coves below. There were also displays of birds of prey put on by a local club, and at some point during the festivities the lifeboat would be launched and a rescue at sea enacted.

The company at the Victoriana were busy rehearsing next week's play during the morning but the afternoon was free for them because it wasn't a matinee day and the evening show didn't start until 7.30. 'And let's face it,' Prince said, 'how many of us are interested in looking at slimy, slippery fish? Me, I like eating them when someone else has taken their innards out and cleaned and cooked them.' Since Arnold's death Prince was more outspoken and confident-sounding than ever, and that fact didn't go unnoticed by several members of the company.

The Climb, as it was advertised, was part of the afternoon entertainment and always drew the crowds. Some gathered on the beach to watch the participants start off and many more waited at the top to see the first heads appear and the competitors scramble over the edge, to be met by the mayor and mayoress and various other dignitaries.

Peter Strong, the men's understudy, was a keen climber and told them he would be taking part.

'Come on, folks, let's all go and support Peter, cheer him on.' Prince's voice took on a rallying note, before he added, 'Mind, I think it's a crazy thing to do, climb up a steep cliff like that, but then there's no accounting for taste, is there? As long as no-one expects me to try anything like it.'

Crystal opted out and went off with tears glistening in her eyes and a sulky expression on her face. Prince Kingly shrugged his shoulders and murmured to Roger, who was standing next to him, 'There'll be plenty of pretty girls up there, I expect. She's the one who'll miss all the fun, not us.'

Tim Merry decided to go home and rest during the afternoon. He had seen it all before and the pressure of the murder enquiry was getting to him. He wished Peter Strong wasn't going to climb — if he slipped and injured or killed himself they'd be another player short, and the man was actually proving quite good in Arnold's parts. He kept these thoughts to himself, however, and simply nodded to Charlie and said 'See you this evening' as he went out.

It turned into a jolly afternoon. Most of the cast were there on the clifftop and chatted together more happily than they had for some time. It was a hot day and the sea below shimmered in the glint of the sun, but on the top of the cliff there was a lovely fresh breeze blowing. Roger moved over to where Betty was standing with Nicola and Prince. 'Mind if I join you?' he said. 'We can all shout encouragement together.'

Feeling light-hearted because Crystal wasn't joining them, Betty gave him a radiant smile. 'You didn't fancy taking part, then, Roger?' she said.

'Not me — cricket's my game. Scaling cliffs and rock climbing just doesn't appeal.'

'Hear, hear,' said Prince. 'I'm with you there. In fact, I'm no sportsman at all — watching's my game, especially in this lovely weather. Sunbathing and, yes, all right, watching the girls go by.' They joined in the laughter and suddenly Nicola said, 'Look, people are going to the edge — they must be starting.' The whole group moved forward and sure enough, far, far below, they could see the climbers spread out at the foot of the cliff. A whistle blew and they were off. It was hard to tell who was who from that distance, but there was a carnival atmosphere as everyone shouted encouragement. The police were in evidence too as they warned people not to get too close to the edge, then the mayoral car arrived and the mayor, mayoress and several more of their party were ushered along to the dais and chairs set up for them in a roped-off area on the grass.

'We chose the right spot to see everything,' Prince said to no-one in particular. 'We can watch them get their medals, then I shall go down to the beach and have a swim before tonight's performance. Anyone want to join me? Nicola? Betty?' An attractive young lady close by said quietly, 'I'm going for a swim after this too — two groins left of the pier is where I'll be. Probably see you there.'

Prince edged closer to her. 'Not probably, definitely,' he said quietly.

Betty followed the little encounter closely and turned to smile at Roger — maybe he too would suggest something similar, but he had moved away a little and was looking through a pair of binoculars he had with him.

When most of the climbers were about halfway, a policeman walked by, warning the crowd to keep well back as they neared the top. Obediently most of them moved a little, only to return to the edge when he was out of sight.

'Can't see anything back there,' Prince said as he moved to join Roger at the brink of the cliff. He was clutching a camera. 'I'll try and get a picture for posterity,' he said.

'I can see Peter now! He's going well!' Roger called out. 'Can you see him? Look, he's more than halfway, I'd say.' Nicola edged closer and looked down on the amazing sight of dozens of people spread out along the cliff, climbing up as if their lives depended on it.

'Careful,' Prince said. He had taken his picture and was standing between her and Betty now. 'We'd better get back, at the speed they're all going they'll be here in a few minutes.'

There were people three deep behind them, which prevented them moving for a few seconds. The policeman had returned and was waving them all to get further back when suddenly a scream pierced the sunny afternoon with fright. There were murmurings from the crowd as people moved away from the edge, many with their hands covering their shocked faces, and as the actors and actresses from the Victoriana grouped together near the mayor's official stand, an ambulance, which had been parked further over, came forward.

'What's happened? Has someone gone over? Was it a climber or one of the crowd?' Prince said, looking rather white faced now the bonhomie of the afternoon had turned to tragedy.

'A spectator,' a woman standing near him said, 'but she didn't go right down — one of the climbers caught her.'

Nicola looked around, mentally checking them all. 'Where's Betty?'

Roger and Prince caught the panic in her voice and suddenly they were searching all the faces milling around. Then they saw the ambulance men carrying a stretcher towards the vehicle, and their own Peter Strong following them. As one they moved across the clifftop. Peter saw them. 'It's Betty!' he called out as he was ushered into the ambulance with her.

'Oh my God. This season's doomed,' Prince muttered. 'Is she — is she alive?' But Peter had disappeared inside and the doors had closed.

The ambulance moved slowly across the bumpy terrain towards the road on the other side of the cliff. The spectators watched, many of them seeming not to know what to do next. The climbers scrambled over the edge and made their way to the mayoral party to receive their medals for completing the climb.

12

Betty was in hospital for two days only. Her injuries were not life threatening because her rescuer Peter Strong had caught her while still managing to hold on to his precarious position on a ledge in the cliff. Those climbing with him had formed a cocoon around them and those coming up behind provided extra protection for Peter. Betty was much shaken and she had a few bruises and scratches and a graze on her cheekbone, probably sustained as she hurtled downwards. She felt extremely stiff but there were no broken bones and, lying in the hospital bed and reliving the nightmare of the fall, she knew it was a miracle that she had survived.

Peter visited her in hospital the following morning, where she broke down as she tried to thank him for saving her life. 'I could have sent you down too,' she said, as she dried her eyes with his large hankie.

'I'm a strong climber, Betty, and a tenacious one, though I must admit I have never had a beautiful woman land in my arms three quarters of the way up a cliff before.'

His words had the desired effect and she

laughed softly with him. 'I've never thrown myself into a man's arms so blatantly before either,' she said. 'But seriously, Peter, thank you so much. And for coming in to see me this morning.'

He told her that Doris, the dresser and understudy for all the women in the play, had taken over her part last night.

'They are going to let me out later after the doctor has seen me,' she said. 'They did a few tests this morning but everything seems to be fine.'

Inspector Carding appeared at this point and Peter said he was just leaving. He took hold of her hand and then, very gently, he leant over the bed and kissed her on the forehead. 'See you later, Betty,' he said.

The inspector waited on a seat in the corridor while the doctor was with Betty and when he was allowed back in not long afterwards, it was to be greeted with the happy news that she was fit to go home.

'I'll take you,' he said. 'It will be more private to talk to you back there too. Just one or two questions, Miss Morse, then I'll leave you to have a quiet few hours before your stint tonight. Or will you have the evening off?'

Betty treated him to a smile. 'You know the old adage, Inspector. The show must go on.

I'll be there on stage tonight.'

Back at her digs, the landlady made a great fuss of Betty. 'What an awful thing to happen,' she said. 'Terrible. I was there but of course I didn't see you, and when somebody said a person had fallen over the cliff I didn't even dream it was you.'

She brought some tea and biscuits up to Betty's room, and clearly would have liked to stay for a while, but John Carding leapt from his chair and opened the door for her to go through while thanking her for the refreshments. 'Just what she needs,' he said quietly, 'and I promise I won't keep her long then she can have some peace and quiet before the show tonight. She is fortunate to have such pleasant and comfortable lodgings.'

Betty smiled as he sat down again. 'You would do well as an actor, Inspector.'

'I doubt I'd be able to keep it up, Miss Morse.' He pitched his voice low and quiet in case the landlady was listening outside the door. 'Miss Morse, can you tell me who was standing next to you when you fell?'

'Yes, Prince and Roger were the closest. Prince had taken a photo of the climbers, and as we all leaned forward to try to see how near they were, I suppose I must have tripped. It's pretty rough ground up there, holes and tufts of grass, and I don't think I had the most suitable type of shoes on. Oh, not very high heels or anything like that, but flimsy summer shoes — you could feel the heat from the ground coming up through them.'

He glanced down at her footwear. 'I see what you mean. You didn't feel any pressure as though someone was pushing you?' He was watching her face closely and noticed a slight hesitation before she answered. 'No, I don't think anyone pushed me, Inspector. There was a crowd there and Roger put his arm round Nicola as she edged forward to see better then we all moved a little as people behind us tried to get nearer. Someone's arm came round me — I don't know if it was Roger or Prince — in a sort of protective way.'

'And then?' he prompted softly.

She covered her face with both hands before she said in a muffled voice. 'Suddenly I was falling. The ground simply wasn't there any more. I — I think I screamed. I really don't remember any more until I heard Peter saying, 'Keep perfectly still and you'll be all right, I have you safe as long as you don't move.'' Slowly she took her hands from her face and looked at him. 'It was an accident, Inspector. We should not have been that close to the edge. The police kept moving us back

157

but I suppose, in the excitement of the moment, we did surge back when they had gone. Everyone did, and it was so easy then for it to happen. I'm surprised a whole crowd of us didn't go over really.'

She had gone quite pale as she talked, and John Carding walked briskly over to the small table with the tea tray on. 'Here, you need a cup of tea and a rest. Sorry to put you through that but I needed to hear it exactly as it was from you.' He poured two cups of tea and handed one to her. 'Sugar?'

'No, thanks. I learnt to do without during the war.' As they sipped their tea he said quietly, 'You are right, you know. It is a wonder that more people didn't go over, isn't it?'

'I suppose so. We were nearest the edge. There was nothing in front of us to stop the fall.'

As he finished his tea and rose to leave he said, 'Who was on your right and who was on your left?'

She tried to answer him but all she could recall was seeing Roger put his arm round Nicola and the wave of jealousy that seared through her as she edged forward. And then, a second or so later, feeling an arm around her. Was it Roger's or Prince's?

'I can't remember,' she said. 'All I

remember is suddenly dropping, suddenly finding no ground beneath me.'

★ ★ ★

Back at the police station, Inspector Carding dealt with a few routine matters then called Sergeant Binns to his office. 'George, I want you to talk to Roger Johnson this afternoon. There's no matinee so I don't know where you'll find him, but I want a statement in his own words about the incident on the clifftop yesterday. I'll do the same with Prince Kingly. Both of those were close to Betty when she toppled off the cliff. See if you can find out who was immediately behind her too, will you? I'm not happy that was a straightforward accident.'

'Yes, chief. Is Betty Morse OK?'

'Yes. She's out of hospital, none the worse for her fall apart from some bruises and grazes which will heal. I've had a chat with her but, understandably, I suppose, she is hazy about exactly what happened. She admits she was right on the edge, and we all know how easily chalk cliffs crumble. But these are designated safe from going into the sea at present. On the other hand, she could have trodden on a bit of loose overhanging turf, and with a crowd behind and around her

159

pushing forward to look over the edge, it is easy to see how there could be an accident.'

'You don't think it was a natural accident, though, chief?'

'I don't know one way or the other, but we do have a murder inquiry going on and Betty Morse is part of that set-up. It's up to us to find out. I wish we knew more about the background of the cast at the Victoriana theatre. If any of them were famous they would be well documented, but none of this lot are. As I said to Ruth the other night, the one most written about is the murdered man's wife, and she was enthralling audiences in Eastbourne when her husband was being killed.'

13

Sergeant Binns found Roger Johnson in the library. The chief knew what he was doing choosing to interview the other one, he thought. Prince was almost certain to be in a prominent position on the beach and easy to find. Roger was a different kettle of fish. He could be anywhere, maybe not even in the town. He tried his digs first, and then systematically worked his way through all the likely places in Fairbourne.

He liked and admired his boss but why the heck couldn't he have organized this for an hour before curtain up or something? George Binns wasn't much of a theatre-going man and didn't know or appreciate the ways of actors.

Roger was looking in the biography section. 'Afternoon,' George said amiably.

'Oh, it's you again. No peace from your lot anywhere, is there?'

'Of course not. This is a murder enquiry we're conducting but that isn't what I want to talk to you about this afternoon. I've been put on checking the accident on the clifftop yesterday. You were there, I understand, Mr Johnson.'

Roger's lips moved slightly and an amused expression flitted across his face. 'Me and several hundred others,' he said.

'I'd like to hear about it in your own words.'

Roger said, 'This is a library, or had you forgotten? The golden rule in libraries is silence.'

'That's fine by me. We can go anywhere you like to talk. Your digs, the seafront, the police station — '

Tight lipped now, Roger said, 'You don't get it, do you? This is also my free time, and I get precious little of that. I too am working.' He indicated the books. 'Doing some research if you must know and my time is important to me.'

'I apologize for the intrusion, of course, but it is a necessary one. So where is it to be? A shelter on the promenade or — '

Roger turned sharply away from the shelf. 'Go on, then, ask your questions, as long as I'm back here within fifteen minutes at the most.'

'That will depend on you, of course. I see no reason why you shouldn't be.'

They left the library together and George turned left to go towards the seafront. Five minutes later they were sitting on a wooden bench, which miraculously no-one else was using. The sergeant took out a small notebook. 'Right, let's start with the time you arrived on the clifftop,' he said.

'Afternoon,' Roger said, his tone sharp.

'Go on. I want to know what you did, where you were standing and who was with you as you watched the climb. It's routine with an incident like this,' the sergeant added, looking at the other man's tight-lipped anger, which showed in every feature and movement of his face and body.

'We were all there watching,' Roger said after a few sullen moments of silence. 'Except Crystal, who said she couldn't bear to feel happy now Arnold was dead, or something like that anyway.'

'And how close to the edge were you?'

'Very close. Stupid, really, but we wanted to see Peter coming up the cliff. Peter Strong, he's the understudy and is playing Arnold's parts now,' he said in a supercilious voice.

'And?'

'And nothing. We could see him, the crowd were pressing in behind us and suddenly there was this scream. We didn't even know it was Betty at first, only that something had happened.'

'But surely Betty was with your group?' George kept his voice low and friendly.

'Yes she was because I spoke to her at one

point earlier on. And to Nicola and Doris — she's the dresser and understudy for the girls.' The sergeant let that go: this man obviously couldn't help lording it over people.

'Anyone else? Who was behind Betty, for instance?'

'How on earth should I know that? We were packed in so tightly you couldn't turn round even if you had wanted to. Let me think. Tim declined to attend. Oh, Prince was there, yes, because he was whizgigging with the girls in his usual casual way. Treats anything in a skirt in an insulting manner. He had his camera with him. Yes, I remember now, he pushed forward to take some pictures of the climbers. I lost track of him after that and of course there was that sudden bloodcurdling scream and — Well, you know the rest.'

'Did you speak to Betty?'

'I can't remember. Probably. We were all talking to each other as I recall. There was a sudden surge from the back as the climbers neared the top — I know Nicola was next to me then because I put my arm round her to keep her safe.'

'So you thought there was a chance of someone falling?'

'That's not what I said, Sergeant Binns. It

was instinct. Even you would probably have done so to protect a lady from the crush. I've told you all I can recall of that afternoon. We can only be thankful it ended well and we didn't lose another player from the cast. Can I get back to my studies now?'

An elderly lady came up to the seat and, smiling sweetly at them, said, 'Is there room for a little one?'

George smiled back at her. 'Of course. We were just going anyway.'

As they rose and walked off he carried on with his questioning. 'As Betty was the person who went over the cliff, it is her position in those last vital minutes I want to ascertain,' he said. 'How long before the scream did you talk to or see her?'

'I've no idea,' Roger replied. 'One doesn't normally take note of things like that on an afternoon out. All I know is that she was there with us all.'

'You said Prince was taking photographs. Did you have your camera with you too, Mr Johnson?'

'I don't have a camera, Sergeant.'

George consulted his rapid shorthand notes. 'You said you spoke to Betty earlier on, and then you said you couldn't remember. Did you speak to her or not, Mr Johnson?'

Roger looked wearily at the sergeant.

'Probably,' he said. 'There was a group of us from the theatre on the cliff and we chatted to each other in between watching the action below. The way you do when you are all in the same place.'

'You all went up together?' George Binns queried.

'No, we went independently but met up there and stayed together in a little bunch during the climb.'

'I see. I presume Betty was standing next to you when you spoke to her? Can you recall if she was to the left or right of you?'

'No, I can't. Both at different times, I suspect. We all moved around when we could.'

George Binns left Roger at the turning that would take him back to the library, while he carried on to the police station.

★ ★ ★

Inspector Carding sauntered along the prom, trying to look like a holidaymaker. Although he was not in uniform he still shrieked policeman. Almost six feet tall, he had a distinct air of authority about him. It was there in his stance, in the way he walked and in his inquisitive hazel eyes. Those eyes took in most things that were happening over a wide range of focus. He noted that the tide was going out and that at least a dozen children were busy making sandcastles. He saw dads with their trousers rolled up, holding the hands of toddlers along the edge of the water, mums paddling and dangling young babies' chubby legs gently into the sea, dancing them up and down so they got the feel of the water from the safety and comfort of familiar arms. He saw the sunbathers dotted between the wooden groins and right out to sea, the movement of the swimmers. The scene took him back years to when his own children were small and the highlight of the year was a week by the sea from their home in Middlesex. That was before the war when he was still climbing the ladder to his exalted position now. Happy days, though, he thought. Not much money but who needs more than this? He stood by the rails for a few moments, drinking in the panorama before him.

He went to where he knew Prince Kingly had a beach hut. It would be bad luck if the actor wasn't there but he was pretty sure he would be. He had made it his business to have an idea where most of the players spent their time when not on stage.

The hut was number 63 and looked like all the others in the line against the seawall.

Many had the door open and you could see crockery and evidence of a snack meal inside, while the occupants were soaking up the sun on deckchairs or loungers by their particular strip of beach. The door of number 63, however, was closed. John Carding knocked loudly. From inside he could hear scuffling and what sounded like a grunting noise. Well, I know what he's doing, he thought, and at least it means he's there. He knocked again, quite heavily.

'All right, all right. Don't break the door down. Who is it anyway?'

'Carding.'

'Bloody hell. What d'you want? Surely it can wait 'til I'm at the theatre this evening. I'm busy.'

John Carding chuckled softly to himself. 'No, it can't wait. I've a report to file. Come on, open up, and hurry.' He almost said. 'Get your pants on and open the door quickly,' but had second thoughts on that. Hardly befitting of an inspector. 'I'll give you three minutes,' he shouted. One or two of the other beach-hut owners were looking towards him now as he stood on the beach outside the hut, looking like a soldier on guard. He heard bolts being drawn back and then Prince Kingly was there beside him. A very angry Prince Kingly.

'I hope you realize you have just spoilt a beautiful romance, Inspector,' he said, all the deference of the first day of interviews gone.

'There'll be another time, I'm sure. Do you want to let her get out so we can talk privately inside?' he said.

A blonde appeared in the doorway and, without looking at either of them, scuttled away down the beach towards the sea.

'I'll see you later, darling, when I've sorted out this little business problem for my colleague here,' he called after her, and Carding couldn't resist a smile for the man's sheer bravado.

'I believe you took some pictures of the climb as they neared the top the other day,' he said when they were seated on two folding chairs inside the hut.

'I did, but haven't had 'em developed yet.'

'No problem. Let me have the film and we'll sort that out for you.'

'They're only photos of people climbing the cliffs and a few views of different parts of Fairbourne. There may be some bathing beauties on it but they're all wearing costumes or bikinis — you won't find any nudes. I told you before, I'm clean. Nothing since that skirmish when I was a lad. Anything else important enough to disturb me for?'

'I'll have you for insolence if you're not careful. Were you at any time standing next to or behind Betty Morse?'

'Of course I was. We were all there in a bunch. But I didn't push anyone over the edge, if that's what you're thinking.'

'I'd like you to try to visualize where everyone was just before the accident.'

Prince let out a deep sigh. 'I wouldn't swear in court to any of this because I wasn't taking a lot of notice, but Nicola, Betty, Doris and me and Roger were certainly up near the edge of the cliff. I do remember Roger leaning over and saying he could see Peter with the front climbers and we all peered over, then I urged the girls to get back. There were people behind us so it wasn't easy but we did manage to get away from the sheer drop. Largely because the police were moving the crowds behind us, I think.'

'You said the girls. Which girls?'

Prince sounded exasperated. 'Doris and her friend, and before you ask, no, I don't know her name. I wasn't introduced to her, but she was there. And Betty and Nicola.'

With an abrupt change of subject, John Carding said, 'Is your camera a good one? I'm interested in photography myself.'

Prince rose from the chair and went over to a duffel bag in the corner of the hut. Diving his hand in, he pulled out a brown camera case. 'Here, you may as well pay for the developing to make up for my ruined afternoon,' he said sharply. 'There's a few left on the reel, I think, so they'll be wasted, but I'd appreciate prints of the rest.'

★　★　★

Back at the station, Inspector Carding checked his notes about Prince Kingly. Then he took a folder from his drawer. In it were records of a certain lad from Hackney called Joe Smith and one of the charges against him was common battery and assault.

14

Something wasn't right somewhere. The inspector knew they were all hiding something and not talking about it, but what was it? How did it affect them all? He couldn't put his finger on it. Maybe it was time for the handwriting test. Carding didn't like turning to this but used sensibly he realized it did help. He wouldn't do it too soon because he felt that it was not true detective work — mumbo jumbo, really. No, not that, but cheating nevertheless. Well, maybe more like putting ideas and reasons on to people which are not there in reality. After all, a deceitful streak could apply to any part of a life, couldn't it, and maybe a few pertinent questions would be answered and he could dismiss a couple of theories that might have other explanations and be nothing whatsoever to do with Arnold Brand's murder. He felt very strongly that he had missed something that was right there in front of him.

He called George Binns into his office the next morning. He had the photographs from Prince's camera on his desk and passed them over for his sergeant to see. George glanced through them all then studied them one by one for a few seconds each.

'Not much there, guv, is there?' he said, handing them back. 'The few from the day in question are so blurred. Can't distinguish anything or anybody. Just some blobs on the cliffside. He's captured Fairbourne well in the others, though. That one of Black Cat Cottage is as good as any on the postcards of it.'

John Carding took them back from his sergeant and shuffled through again, stopping at the cottage one. 'Yes, it is. There are some great pics here, as you say. Quite a photographer, is our Mr Kingly.'

'The bathing beauties are lovely — that's the sort of photography I would expect from him, mind,' George Binns said with a grin.

'But all with costumes on, as he told me,' the inspector replied. 'He thought we were looking to catch him out in pornography. No, what bothers me about this case, George, is the lack of leads. All these people who detested Arnold Brand, yet none of them seem to have a strong enough motive to kill him. We're missing something. So what did you make from their handwriting skills? What does it tell you about them, George?'

Sergeant Binns put the handwriting samples on his boss's desk and took a small notebook from his breast pocket. 'Any particular order?' he asked.

'No, as they come.'

'The one that shows more stress than any other is Tim Merry. We know he's a natural worrier and when he wrote this he, like the others, had had a tremendous shock. Would be interesting to see a sample of his writing in, say, a letter to a friend on a good day. Look at those falling lines and the heavy pressure on the downward strokes. He's probably a depressive and he's certainly a perfectionist. Now this one — who would you say this is, sir? This is what I've written down: *Ambitious, outgoing, strong sexual imagination*.'

'And a bit wild in his youth, or doesn't that show? Our little Prince, is it?'

'It certainly is. There is an aggressiveness there — both the g and the y tails are fairly heavily filled in on his surname.'

'A record of assault and battery in his youth and he was close enough to Betty to give that extra push that sent her over the cliff,' John Carding said. 'But, then, so were several others. Go on, George.'

'Betty Morse reveals stress and tension, and great sensitivity, and Nicola Coates shows attention to detail and exceptional control.'

'Exceptional control? In what area, George? Does it mean over her emotions or is she a controlling type of person?'

'Can't tell from this. A real expert probably could, but her control is *very* strong according to this writing,' George said.

'Right. A lady with hidden depths, maybe, because she doesn't strike one like that from her appearance or demeanour, does she?'

'That's true, but as you know, guv, this needs to be balanced with so many other aspects and conditions. But I'd be willing to bet she's more strong-minded than she appears to be.'

'What about the others, George? Who have we got left?'

'Crystal Holman and Roger Johnson.'

'Right, fire away then.'

'Roger seems to be an organized person. His writing suggests calm and orderly behaviour but an indifferent sort of emotional response. Not the sort of man to fall in love at first sight and throw his cap over the windmill, you know.'

'Poor Betty,' the inspector said. 'That's what I think she is hoping he will do.'

George glanced down at his list. 'That leaves Crystal because I haven't got some of the others. She is not as emotionally unstable as she seems, according to her writing. Large sexual appetite and there is anger showing in her sample as well as frustration and some insecurity. An interesting one, actually, because even in this short sample there are many conflicting emotions.'

'Thanks, George. Maybe I'll talk to Nicola Coates again, find out where this control that shows up so strongly in her handwriting fits in. Maybe to do with her personal life but it could be that we are taking her too much at face value. This murder isn't going to be solved before Superintendent Salk returns from his conference, I'm afraid, which lets us in for it.'

'We haven't found anyone outside the theatre yet who Brand was blackmailing,' Sergeant Binns said, 'but then they are hardly likely to come forward of their own accord, are they, guv?'

'Not if they've got any sense. I wish we knew more about the cast's stage lives and their private lives. You can often tell if a bunch of ordinary people are acting but it's more difficult with a group of actors and actresses. Harder to tell if they are concealing anything when they earn their living doing just that — acting and making it seem real. Of course, if they are it may not be to do with the murder. People often have secrets they don't want known; we've unearthed a few these last few days. Pity they're not famous. They'd be well documented then, but this lot are simply jobbing thespians. The one most written about, as I said the other day, is the murdered man's wife and she isn't even in the play. But Iris Brand had plenty of motive, George. We know she wants to marry her lover. Let's presume Arnold wouldn't consider divorce because he needed his wife's money. He was a vain and greedy man after all. She'd need a hitman — '

'Or woman.'

'Yes, or woman, and of course she has the perfect alibi because she was on stage somewhere else at the time of the murder.'

Sergeant Binns returned his notebook to his pocket.

'Are those notes in shorthand, George?' John Carding asked.

'Yes, sir, and in my own version of shorthand too, which is slightly different from Pitmans or Greggs. Only I can decipher these.'

'Good man.'

15

Inspector Carding called on Tom Holman during the Wednesday matinee when he knew Crystal would not be there. Holman was far from welcoming.

'What is it now?' he said. 'Still trying to find out who killed that obnoxious man, are you?'

'It is our job to do just that, Mr Holman. Now, I have a few questions you can supply answers to, so may I come inside or shall we do the job here on the doorstep?'

'You had better come in, I suppose, but I hope this isn't going to take long. I have two appointments this afternoon as well as a lot of work to get through. In here.' He opened a door on the left of the hall. It was not as large as the study they had been into on the last occasion, and was furnished as a sitting room, with two royal blue two-seater sofas and a couple of dark blue leather armchairs. In one corner was a chintz-covered rocking chair and dotted around at intervals were several small coffee tables. A long, low, glass-topped table with a filled bowl of fruit standing on a cream-coloured lace mat was the centrepiece of the room.

Tom Holman sat in one of the armchairs and waved his arm towards the other for his obviously unwelcome guest. 'Well?'

'You lied to me the other day when you said you didn't own a gun. I find you have what might be described as a set of them and that you are a member of a gun club in London and have won prizes for your prowess with shooting. Why did you lie?'

'Look, I didn't kill that wretched man. My conscience is clear so why should I tell you all my business?'

'You told us very little. In fact, I could probably have you for withholding information. Apart from bloody-mindedness, why did you conceal your membership? You must have realized we would find out.'

Tom smirked. Not a pleasant expression but it was the first time the inspector had seen him look pleased about anything at all.

'Might not have been bloody-mindedness. Could have been because I didn't wish to show off or even to be thought that I was showing off.'

'Look, Mr Holman, stop playing games with me. You not only had access to guns but you are a crack shot. Your wife was having an affair with the victim, who was also holding you to ransom over something you didn't want known in general circles — '

'It was an accident!' Tom shouted, his face flushing dangerously. 'Everyone accepted that it was. The bloody chap shouldn't have got in the way of the guns. He wasn't killed or even badly hurt, a mere graze, and all his own fault . . . All right, I'll tell you about it. He was a relative newcomer to the shoots, not genuine at all, just a social climber. Enjoyed flirting with the women back at the house later. No-one liked him but it was an accident. There was never any suggestion it was anything more. Everyone accepted that.'

John Carding hid his surprise well. 'Was there any reason it might be other than accidental?' he said.

'No. I told you. The man wasn't safe to be let out with grown men.'

'I presume he was a member of a club so he would have known how to behave when guns were present?' Carding said.

'Wasn't a member of our club. It was the only time we let him come. One of the others had asked to bring him. Damned embarrassing all round, but as I said it was no-one's fault but his own.'

'Yes, I understand that. Tell me, was your wife one of the women he flirted with, Mr Holman?'

'He made eyes at them all; Crystal no more

than the others. He was like a fish out of water — suddenly had a bit of money and fancied himself as a toff. Got in everyone's way.' The steam seemed to go out of him suddenly. 'I should have told you, of course, but as it had nothing to do with this case I thought it wouldn't crop up. I ought to have known you would check on clubs and guns. Very short-sighted of me.'

John Carding said, 'How much were you paying Arnold Brand to keep it to himself?'

'A tenner a week. Didn't even miss it. Even felt sorry for the poor sod if he was earning so little he had to resort to that sort of tactic. What sort of an actor was that?'

'Anything else you want to tell me, now you have decided to come clean and help instead of hinder, Mr Holman?'

Tom Holman looked genuinely surprised. 'No, that's the only skeleton in my cupboard, Inspector,' he said.

'What sort of books did you say you wrote, sir?'

'Westerns. Everyone knows that. You saw them in my study the last time you came.'

'That's right, I did. You stick to the one genre then, I gather? A western specialist.'

Tom Holman said, 'Yes. It's interesting and it pays well. I have a huge army of fans who devour my books.'

'Have you ever written any about the war?'

'No.'

'So how did you come by a collection of World War Two guns? British and German.' He indicated a glass-fronted cabinet on the opposite wall which he spotted as soon as he walked in.

'I was going to write about the war and I saw this collection advertised so I bought it for research purposes. I changed my mind and decided to stick with the cowboys.'

'But you kept the collection. Why?'

Tom Holman's short burst of goodwill appeared to be running out. 'Because I'd paid for it and it looked good in the cabinet,' he said tersely.

Inspector Carding rose and walked over to the mahogany and glass cabinet. There were ten small guns displayed but not a Luger among them and no spaces where one might have been.

'If you think of anything that might help this investigation, you know where to contact me, Mr Holman.' He rose and went towards the door.

★ ★ ★

'I've found a victim Brand missed,' Inspector Carding said to his sergeant when he got back

182

to the police station. 'He *was* blackmailing Tom Holman but not over keeping the romance books quiet — it was over a shooting incident that happened a few years ago.' He laughed. 'Strange, isn't it?' He's managed to keep Hearts and Flowers secret but Brand found out about the shooting accident, and I think it really was an accident, and he was paying him the usual tenner for his silence. Dismissed it as though it was a tanner but if Brand had known about the other it would have been double at least and I'm not sure what might have happened then. I checked cameras with him but he said he doesn't own one.

'Leave all that publicity stuff to my publishers,' he told me. ''Most ordinary people can't take a decent picture anyway. You see them waving their tiny cameras around and wasting their money on mostly blurred snapshots instead of going to a professional and having a proper job done.''

'That sounds like Tom Holman,' Sergeant Binns said.

'I don't know what his writing is like but his acting isn't bad and he's a pretty good liar too. All this makes him a strong suspect, George. Brand was blackmailing him over one thing he desperately wanted to keep quiet about, which involved guns, and there was always the danger that he would find out about the romance books too. But apart from that his wife was Brand's current lover and although he professed not to care about that, he wouldn't want to look a fool in the town. I suspect only the players knew about the Wednesday and Saturday liaisons in the dressing room and I somehow think it suited Tom Holman and kept Crystal off his back.' His entire face creased into a huge grin. 'In more ways than one.'

George laughed, then he said seriously, 'On circumstantial evidence he's in the top category of suspects, isn't he, chief?'

'Yes, but I don't believe he'll do a runner. There's too much at stake for him. I think, that, if he's our man, he'll brazen it out. It adds up on every count bar one. He had a motive and he had the expertise. I'm sure he would have access to a Luger too with his connections. And he is devious enough not to use the type of weapon he writes about nor collects. He is a good plotter, his job ensures that. It's true that he has no proof that he was at home during the crucial time but, then, we have no proof that he wasn't.'

The inspector wasn't smiling now and George said quietly, 'You said every count bar one, chief?'

'I did. It's this. If Tom Holman murdered his wife's lover and if Charlie Ferguson is speaking the truth, then how did he get in and out of the theatre without being seen?'

16

Betty Morse pulled back the curtains and looked out of her bedroom window. The sky was a blaze of pink glory; it was going to be a beautiful day. If only she could spend some of it with Roger. But everything in that direction seemed to be going wrong lately. At the beginning of the season they had gravitated towards each other so naturally. His kisses when he took her back to her digs stirred emotions in her which she thought had died with Chen. It wasn't just the physical side; they were on the same wavelength about books and films and walking, and she had begun to hope that when they left Fairbourne at the end of the summer there would be further developments.

Not that he had actually asked her to marry him — and for Roger she knew it had to be marriage or nothing. She liked this trait in him. It was unusual among the men she had met but that didn't make it undesirable. I'm reading more into this than is there, she thought, trying to be practical.

Later she walked down to the phone box on the corner and telephoned her mother in

London. 'How is Lillee?' she asked.

'Fine, Betty. It's such a lovely day I'm taking her to the park this afternoon to feed the ducks. She loves that. How's the play going, my love?'

'Full house every night. Of course, there's this murder hanging over us. Frankly I'll be glad when the season's finished.'

'Have the police got no further?'

'How can you tell? They keep popping in and out, asking a lot of questions, but they've not made an arrest yet. I'd hate to think it was one of the company, Mum.' She shivered and her voice tailed away.

'Much more likely for someone outside the theatre to have done it,' her mother said. 'After all, you all know each other.'

Betty smiled rather grimly to herself at this piece of logic as she was walking back. Her mother knew nothing of Arnold Brand's threats, of course, and she had no intention of telling her. She realized it gave her a motive for killing him and she was worried that in spite of his kind words, Inspector Carding might still release her story, or part of it, to the press.

She pictured Lillee feeding the ducks in the park, her solemn little face and beautiful dark eyes lighting up with pleasure as she had seen them do before. Maybe this Sunday, if Roger didn't want her company, she would go home and see her.

It had begun so well with Roger but the last few weeks had been very unhappy. And strangely, she reflected, he hadn't gone off her for Nicola, as seemed likely at first, but for Crystal.

She made herself a snack lunch and went for a long walk on the seafront. She tried to keep her thoughts away from Arnold Brand's murder but it forced its way in and eventually she gave up and let the events of the past few days chatter in her mind.

She was glad Arnold was dead — the fact that the man she loved and the man who could have killed his affection for her had shared a dressing room had been a constant source of worry. She supposed she had been foolish to go to Crystal's room and ask her to lay off Roger. She hadn't gone with that intention but when Roger asked her to return the borrowed books to Crystal it seemed an ideal opportunity and she took it. Recalling Crystal's reaction now, she wondered if the woman was really trying to distract from her own trysts with Arnold. Maybe that and Crystal's conviction that she was so attractive no man could resist her. Perhaps Roger had simply been his normal charming self and Crystal had led him on. Another thought suddenly occurred — what if he was trying to put *her* off and prove that he was free to go around with anyone, even a married woman? That fact, Crystal's marital status, had puzzled her, given Roger's forthright views on ethical behaviour. Was it possible that he did it because he knew nothing more could come of being seen occasionally with Crystal, and as a warning to others in the cast, herself and Nicola in particular, that he wanted no commitment? Was the fact that she had been his date more than the others frightening him off so he had decided to cool it?

The sea was calm and sparkling in the warm sun and as she paused and looked over the railings at the children splashing about at the water's edge, and the mums and dads spread-eagled on beach towels or in deck-chairs, she felt a deep regret for what she was missing.

After Chen died and Lillee was born, she had devoted her life to her child, but she had felt grateful so many times for her mother's insistence that Lillee be brought up as *her* adopted child.

'After all,' her mother had argued, 'you might some day meet someone else, and you don't want to start with a handicap when it can be avoided.'

Tears had filled her eyes as she said, 'Lillee

is *not* a handicap, mum.'

Closing her eyes now Betty recalled the feel of her mother's hand on hers as she said, 'Sorry, darling. Bad choice of word. I didn't mean it that way.'

The arrangement had worked well. Lillee knew she lived with her grandma because her mother had to work away. There was no confusion in the little girl's mind. She lived a settled life and Betty felt thankful and comforted.

Until she met Roger, Betty hadn't wanted anyone else, and for the first few weeks she had thought he felt the same and that they were going to pick up where they had left off at the end of last year's tour.

She returned home about five o'clock, washed and changed and walked down to the theatre well before she needed to. She often did this because if Roger was early too, they would have time for a cuppa together in the cafe opposite. They had done this once during the first week of being in Fairbourne, and she knew he often went in there. Maybe there would be a chance to recapture some of the camaraderie they'd had before he started playing the field. She wondered again if she had been too obvious with her attentions and frightened him off to the extent that he felt there was safety in numbers. Her thoughts returned to last year and her hopes at the end of that season. While she knew deep within herself that she would never love again in the way it had been for her and Chen, she also realized she wasn't a natural loner. She needed a man, both physically and emotionally. She had been drawn to Roger from their first meeting, he was intelligent, presentable, but most of all he stirred feelings in her that had lain dormant for several years.

She was roughly equal distance from her lodgings and the Victoriana, and about halfway across the road, when she heard the screech of a car unmistakably travelling much too fast. There was absolutely nothing she could do. Her eyes registered a flash of white as terror gripped her, yet in that split second before impact she instinctively ducked. The car raced on, leaving her lying motionless in the road.

17

'Carding here.' His expression showed no visible change as he said into the telephone receiver, 'Yes, yes, which hospital? Right, I'll be there if you want me.'

'Betty Morse has been run over,' he told Sergeant Binns as he strode through the outer office. 'Drive me to the Buckland Hospital as fast as you can. That was the traffic officer,' he said as they headed to the car. 'Hit and run. When he realized who the accident victim was he contacted me.'

There were two hospitals in Fairbourne but the Buckland was the one with a casualty department, and as the police car turned into the car park the inspector looked sombre.

They were directed to an upstairs ward where a pretty Irish sister took them into her office and said in an attractive voice, 'Miss Morse is in a critical condition and is unconscious, Inspector. I gather it was a hit-and-run driver. Well, between you and me he may have done for the girl, but we will pull her through if it's humanly possible. If she regains consciousness and the doctors agree, would you like me to let you know so you can talk to her?'

'Yes, please, Sister. It's extremely important. She may have known who knocked her down.'

'Very well.'

The inspector rose. 'If she should say anything, however muddled or crazy it may seem, would you let me know, Sister?'

'Sure I will. But it's going to be some while before that young woman talks, I'm afraid — if ever,' she added softly.

★　★　★

Back at the station, John Carding asked for the report of the accident.

'White Ford Anglia, abandoned in the station yard. It's a hired car, and DC Jones is working round the hire firms now.'

'He may not have hired it in Fairbourne,' George Binns said.

'We'll soon know, although it's unlikely to tell us who really hired it.'

'He'd have to have shown a licence.'

'Could have stolen one.'

'You think this hit and run *is* to do with Arnold Brand's murder, chief? Not simply an accident?'

'Yes, I do. There's the cliff accident and now this. Someone, and it looks as though it was Betty, knows something and hasn't yet told us, and the killer is going to make damn sure they don't. Thing is, who else knows whatever Betty knew?'

'Someone wanted Crystal implicated too, chief — that prop gun in her room. It's hardly a time for playing practical jokes when one of your colleagues gets murdered, is it?'

'Exactly. Why? There's a lot I don't get about this case, George. Undercurrents that — '

The telephone rang on his desk and he answered it quickly. 'Welsh — I see. OK. That'll be all for the moment, thanks.' He pursed his lips into a soundless whistle as he replaced the receiver.

'The name of the man who hired the Ford Anglia is Welsh. What do you make of that, George?'

'Gloria Welsh's father? The old lady's husband? But I thought she was a widow?'

'Someone could have stolen her husband's driving licence. They're not automatically impounded when someone dies. You'd better get over to the garage he hired it from and try to get a description. It's the Loop Garage in Eastbourne. If they're closed, find out where the manager lives and contact him there if you can.'

When George Binns had left, Inspector

Carding telephoned the hospital, before returning to the theatre to see Tim Merry.

'It's bad news, I'm afraid,' he told the manager. 'Betty Morse was run over this evening and is in a critical condition.'

'Betty! God, whatever next?' His voice was distraught and husky. 'Critical, you say? Will she recover, do you think, Inspector?'

'Who can tell? It looks grim though. What did you do when she didn't turn up?'

'Doris went on. They'll be off for the interval soon — they're all a bit nervy, what with Arnold's murder and Betty not being here tonight. I rang her lodgings and her landlady said she left about five, so we had to presume something untoward had happened to her.'

He didn't tell Carding about the absolute panic backstage immediately after his call when he told the cast that she had left her lodgings at the usual time. His own thoughts had echoed most of theirs — had she done a runner? Was she Arnold Brand's killer and getting out before the police came for her?

'Do you know much about her background, Mr Merry? We have to let her folks know.'

Tim literally shook himself back to the present moment, the blurred images of the cast's faces as they gazed at him still more real than the man now standing before him. He felt a band of pain wrap itself around his head as he tried to focus on the inspector's face. It took a few moments for him to speak and his voice had the tremor of shock in it as he said, 'Betty Morse. Not really. A mother who lives in London, I believe. She sometimes used to go up immediately after the Saturday evening show. I presume she stayed for the weekend, but she was always back here in time on Mondays. Apart from that I've no idea. Nicola may be able to help — they share a dressing room.'

'I know. Could I see her in the interval?'

Two expressions flitted simultaneously across his ashen face: panic and fright.

'If you must, I suppose, Inspector, but couldn't it wait until the end? Everyone's on edge as it is.'

John Carding looked at his watch. He knew the traffic division would have already contacted her relatives. It was their job in the circumstances but it was a good ruse to see how much some of the others knew.

'All right. I'll probably be able to get her home address from her landlady anyway. Everyone else arrive at the proper time tonight, Tim?'

'Yes.' He nodded worriedly. 'Poor Betty. Poor, poor girl.' Shaking his head again he added, 'We're only halfway through the season — whatever else is going to happen?'

★ ★ ★

Betty's landlady couldn't help with the home address. 'A very private young lady,' she said. 'Kept herself to herself, not like some of 'em. She never gossiped with me — always pleasant but never chattered about anything except the theatre and books, that sort of thing. I did ask her once if she'd always wanted to go on the stage, and she said yes, ever since she was a little girl. She used to go around with Roger Johnson sometimes — he lodges with a friend of mine, if you want that address — although just lately they seem to be going their separate ways. He may know her home address though. Oh, it does seem a shame, such a nice young lady, and a good actress too. I always go on the Monday night to see the play — I get complimentary, you see . . . '

John Carding telephoned his wife to say he would be late, and George Binns rang to say he had seen the manager of the car hire firm but he hadn't served Peter Welsh himself, and the assistant who had would be there in the morning.

'OK, George. Go and see him first thing,

will you? And get off home now before your wife divorces you for desertion, eh?'

'Thanks, chief. Good night.'

Then John Carding returned to the Victoriana. Nicola Coates was upset when she heard the news about Betty, but she couldn't help with an address.

'She used to go to London sometimes to see her family, but she never talked about them — not to me, anyway. We aren't really pals.' She smiled at him uncertainly. 'But this is awful. I — suppose it's — just an accident, Inspector. Nothing to do with the murder, I mean?'

'We don't know yet,' he replied slowly, watching her face. 'Do you have reason to believe it might be?'

'Oh no, no, of course not.' She looked flushed now. 'I don't know what made me say that really.'

'You're sure, Miss Coates?'

She nodded and tears came into her eyes. 'Honestly, Inspector. It's the sort of thing you wonder, I suppose, when you're working in a mystery play and then suddenly there's murder and mystery all around you too.'

Roger knew Betty's London address, and the inspector wrote it down even though he had it anyway from that first interview.

'Are you in touch with her family at all, Mr Johnson?'

'No.'

'Yet you have her address?'

'We went out sometimes. We were in a play together last year and exchanged addresses, but I never went to her home,' he said softly.

'Then you met again down here?' the inspector prompted, his voice questioning.

'That's right.'

'What time did you arrive at the theatre this evening, Mr Johnson?'

'About six or just after, I think it was. I often come early and have a cuppa across the road, but I went on to the front for half an hour or so, it being such a fine evening.'

'Do you drive?'

'I do, but I haven't a car down here. Nowhere to keep it.'

'And in London?'

'There's a row of mews garages behind my flat in Victoria. One of them belongs to a friend and I rent it from him.'

'What about his car?'

'He hasn't one at present — uses the garage as a workshop and store but he doesn't want to give it up. They're like gold dust in town. This way it's earning for him and I get somewhere for my car that is relatively cheap.'

Crystal was more fluttery than ever. 'How I've worked tonight I'll never know,' she said. 'First finding the gun in my room, and now — now Betty's accident. It's awful.' Her huge blue eyes filled with tears, and John Carding said briskly as he made for the door, 'Yes, well, we shall soon trace the motorist who injured Betty. Meanwhile, as I mentioned before, don't tell anyone the gun was found in your room.'

'Not . . . even . . . Tom,' she whispered tearfully.

The inspector pictured Tom Holman, big, silent and uncooperative, and allowed himself a tiny smile.

'You may tell your husband if it will relieve you, Mrs Holman,' he said, knowing she would probably have told him anyway, 'but it is important that you don't tell anyone else.' He saw the fear in her eyes and knew he had got his message across.

There was no more that could usefully be done that night and he went home with the niggly thought that the murderer was still one step ahead of him. With so many wanting Arnold out of the way, a clear motive had not emerged in his reasoning yet. That it was a planned crime he didn't doubt, and with this latest development he wondered if Betty had unwittingly stumbled on something which could give the killer away, or if she had known all along who it was and had threatened to tell. But if so, he thought, then why did she not do so at the start?

The person she was closest to in the company was Roger Johnson, and lately he had been paying court to Crystal, if the gossip was to be believed. That would tie up with Betty trying to implicate Crystal, but not with someone trying to murder Betty. Unless she saw who put the gun into Crystal's room; that could account for the need to get rid of her, and satisfactorily explain why she hadn't previously mentioned anything. No-one apart from the police yet knew it wasn't the gun that killed Arnold Brand — only the murderer knows that, Carding thought, but he or she will know that the police are still looking for the Luger and the guilty person must now surely be sweating. That was what he wanted because that was when they were likely to make a mistake that would convict them, he thought grimly.

But if I had gone down to the theatre immediately on receipt of that phone call this morning, instead of waiting until the place was open and hoping it would make the culprit jittery, maybe Betty would not be lying unconscious in the hospital now.

His wife brought him a cup of tea. 'Why

don't you go to bed and sleep on the problem?' she said.

He started, and she laughed. 'I spoke to you twice, then I went out and made the tea, and I swear you didn't even notice I had gone.'

'Sorry, Ruth. I am a bit worried. If I can't find something out soon Salk will be on my back and we'll have to call in the big boys, who'll moan because the trail's gone cold. Anyway, I don't want to do that.'

'No leads at all?' she asked softly.

'Nothing conclusive. They've all either got alibis or weren't in the building at the time. But it's all too pat, Ruth, too neat — and Brand was blackmailing several of them.'

'An overdose of motives.'

'You could say that.' He raised a smile. 'Look, if you wanted to get rid of a gun, what would you do with it?'

She thought for a moment. 'Living here, I'd throw it in the sea,' she said. 'Probably from the end of the pier, or better still from a boat well out in the Channel.'

'The murderer may have done just that, of course, because he, or she, planted a stage prop gun in Crystal Holman's dressing room long after it had been searched. Wiped all fingerprints off, if there were any on it, then phoned us to make sure we found it.'

'Her husband,' she said. 'The writer. Revenge is a powerful emotion, and he could kill two birds with one stone, so to speak. Get rid of his wife's lover, and of her too without drawing suspicion on to himself.'

'He wasn't seen near the theatre.'

'He could have got someone there to do it. Perhaps one of them is his girlfriend?'

'That's a thought,' he said. 'But who? Betty! So he had to get rid of her. Possible, but not probable. I haven't told you that Betty Morse was knocked down on her way to the theatre this evening — by a car which didn't stop.'

'Is she . . . '

'No, she's not dead — yet. She might well be by morning.'

Ruth Carding walked over and put her arms round her husband's shoulders. 'Leave it and come to bed now,' she said. 'You're bound to be fresher after a night's sleep.' Looking at the clock on the mantelpiece she added, 'Or even half a night!'

* * *

Inspector Carding's first job when he reached his office the following day was to telephone the hospital. Betty Morse was alive but unconscious still.

For half an hour he dealt with other matters on his patch, and then he rang Paddington Police Station and asked them to check on Mr Welsh's driving licence.

'I want to know who has it now, and when Mr Welsh died, please.'

Sergeant Binns arrived in the office just after eleven.

'Well, George?'

'I saw Barry Chichester who dealt with that particular car hire,' he said, 'and I've got a description of Mr Welsh — or the man calling himself Mr Welsh, chief.'

'Does it tally with anyone?'

George shook his head. 'Not on the surface. It's not a very good description. Barry Chichester said he hadn't looked much at the chap — it was simply routine. Everything was in order. He showed me a copy of the form car hirers have to fill in — I've got it here.'

'Good man.' John Carding scanned the form his sergeant handed over. 'Peter Welsh . . . ' His eyes roved quickly through the formalities of name and address, printed as these things usually are, and focused on the signature at the end. 'How does *that* tie in with your graphology, George?' he asked.

'Hard to tell with a signature and nothing to compare it with. Barry Chichester said it was the same as the signature on the licence, which was all he was bothered about. And as you see he put 'Imperial Hotel, Eastbourne, Sussex' on it. He wasn't asked, but if he had been I guess he'd have said he was on holiday. I did, of course, check the hotel, but there's no-one of that name there, either as a guest or staff.'

'And the description?'

'Average height, medium build. The nearest I could pin him down to was for him to say that he thought Mr Welsh was a bit shorter than me. I'm five foot ten, so say five foot eight or nine. He wore glasses, grey flannels and a light-coloured jacket. Couldn't remember anything distinctive about the chap at all.'

'What sort of glasses — and frames?'

'I asked him that one. 'Ordinary,' he said. He *thought* the frames were brown. He also came up with brown hair, but I think he couldn't recall the chap well and said it to get rid of me.'

'So he produced the licence, signed the form, and drove the car away to kill Betty Morse.'

'Is she . . . ' George Binns looked at his boss.

'No, but I'm sure he intended to kill her. I've put out an appeal for witnesses. The ambulance men said a crowd had gathered, as they do on these occasions, and several of them said the car was coming much too fast. It's not a busy road, but you need to cross it to get to the theatre unless you take the seafront route. I'm hoping some of these people will come forward.'

'Those who came out of their houses wouldn't have seen anything — he was gone by then — but there must have been a few walking along the pavement to have commented on the speed. PC Walker from traffic control got there as she was being lifted into the ambulance, but the crowd had drifted away.'

'If she recovers, and if we presume it wasn't an accident, then she is still in danger, chief.'

'No-one is allowed in. Sister Murphy is going to telephone if there is any change or if she says anything at all. I haven't the manpower here to put a man on round-the-clock duty but am arranging for a police guard in her room during visiting times. It's unlikely, in any case, that she saw her would-be killer.' He pulled a piece of paper towards him and made some rapid drawings.

'This is where it happened. Betty came down here.' He turned the sheet of paper round. 'Presumably she looked both ways here — ' He stabbed his finger at the crossroads at the end of the road ' — and started to cross. Suddenly, wham, she was lying in the road — and if there was no car in sight when she started to cross, and I don't think there could have been — he could have gone in almost any direction after that for a few minutes. The car was found an hour later in the railway station yard, properly parked, but unlocked and with the keys left in the ignition, and devoid of all fingerprints.'

'He could have walked into the booking office and bought a ticket to London without arousing any suspicion.'

'Or Worthing, or Brighton, or Eastbourne ... DC Jones has checked at the station — nothing there. They've dozens of people travelling from here at that time of night and at this time of year.'

'He could still be here in Fairbourne, watching to see if Betty recovers and remembers what — or who — hit her.'

'I think that's more likely.'

'Why, chief?'

'I think this thing's centred around the Victoriana. Whoever hired that car knew her route, knew where she'd cross, had probably been watching on other evenings. He, or she, is either in the pay of the murderer or else is Arnold Brand's murderer.'

'One of the cast?'

'Or their spouses, lovers or hangers-on.

207

Whoever it is — if it is one of them, will have to stay until the end of the season if they don't intend to be caught. After that, well, we can't watch them all once they've dispersed as a company.' He opened the drawer of his desk and took out the pad with the cast's addresses on. 'I'm going to the hospital now to see her mother, Mrs Morse — Sister rang just before you came in to say she was there. Study these and see what you come up with, George, and I'll meet you in the Red Lion at 1.30 and buy you a beer and a sandwich. OK?'

'OK, chief.'

★ ★ ★

Betty Morse's mother turned out to be tall, thin and elegantly dressed. John Carding didn't know why he was surprised because Betty was very like her, yet he had a picture in his mind of a small, chubby, motherly woman. She was in the little ward nearest Sister's office, quietly sitting by her daughter's bedside, as still as if she were asleep.

'It's all right, Sister, I'll introduce myself,' he said. 'Is it in order to talk to her in there or not?'

'It'll be the most private place, Inspector,

and the poor colleen won't be worried by it yet.'

'How is she?'

'In a deep coma. Hearing her mother's voice might help.'

He thanked her and went into the ward, deliberately walking to the opposite side of the bed so as not to come up behind Mrs Morse and startle her.

'I'm Detective Inspector Carding,' he said quietly when she saw him. 'This is a bad business, Mrs Morse.'

The woman's eyes filled with tears. 'I'm sorry, Inspector. Did — did you want to talk to me?'

'Please. Sister said we could stay here — that in fact it might be good for your daughter to hear voices.'

She opened her handbag and took out a clean handkerchief to dab at her eyes. 'I only know what the policeman and the doctor here have told me,' she said. 'That Betty was knocked down on her way to work, by a car that didn't stop.'

'That's right. But we shall find the driver of that car, never fear.'

She smiled sadly at him. 'But it won't bring my Betty back.'

He looked at the still form on the bed. 'Don't give up hope,' he said quietly. 'She's young and strong. Do you feel like answering one or two questions for me? It could help greatly in our pursuit of the man who did this to Betty.'

'I'll do my best,' she said.

'When did you last see or hear from your daughter, Mrs Morse?'

'Yesterday morning. She telephoned — she usually does several times a week.'

'Does the name of Arnold Brand mean anything to you?' He watched her eyes, which were so like her daughter's, but saw no fear in them.

'He was the man who was murdered last week, wasn't he?'

'That's right.'

The implication seemed to hit her suddenly. 'You don't mean — no — you don't think it was — was the same person who knocked Betty down? You *do*, don't you? You think this was a deliberate — that someone *wanted* to kill Betty. My God — there must be a madman at large.'

'Now, Mrs Morse, we don't know. It could be absolute coincidence that your daughter is the victim of a hit-and-run driver, but we cannot rule out the idea that she may have stumbled on something that could identify Arnold Brand's killer.'

'And he could strike again, when he knows

he didn't — ' she looked at the girl in the bed ' — didn't *quite* kill her.'

'So if you think of anything that might help, you'll contact me at the police station here, Mrs Morse?'

'Yes,' she said, close to tears again.

'Where are you staying?' he asked, more gently.

'I'm going back this evening. I have . . . commitments at home and I can't stay overnight until I've made some arrangements.'

'For Lillee, your little Chinese orphan,' he said. 'Betty told me about her, and how fond she is of her.'

She looked startled. 'Yes, she is,' she said slowly.

In all the time they were talking there had been no movement from the girl lying so still she might almost have been dead. The inspector moved towards the door.

'Does the name Peter Welsh mean anything to you?' he said.

'No.'

'You're sure?'

'Positive. But that doesn't mean that Betty didn't know someone called that. She's twenty-five, lives and works away from home, and although she mentions different friends and colleagues from time to time, she probably knows many I've never heard of.'

'Of course. Goodbye, Mrs Morse. We'll do everything we can.'

★ ★ ★

'I think I'll take Ruth to the theatre tonight,' John Carding said to his sergeant when they were settled in a corner of the Red Lion at lunchtime. 'It's a long while since we saw a play and I want to assess from a distance what any of the men would look like in brown framed glasses. Did the chappie at the garage mention any sort of accent?'

'No. And when he didn't come up with anything like that voluntarily I asked if he thought Mr Welsh was English, Welsh, Irish or Scottish, posh, Cockney . . . he said he sounded just like me!'

'Our bogus Peter Welsh took cover in ordinariness, didn't he? I don't think Mrs Morse knew that Arnold Brand was black-mailing Betty either. Poor girl probably didn't want to worry her mother. Come on, George, back to work.'

18

The following morning was very hot and John Carding was standing by his window and looking down on to the busy police yard when there was a knock on his door. He turned from the window. 'Morning, George,' he said. 'You look warm.'

'There's a heatwave going on outside, chief. I've just had Paddington Station on the blower. They sent someone to see Mrs Welsh about that licence, but she doesn't know where it is. Apparently her husband died last year, so it's been kicking around for twelve months.'

'Just our luck. Could have been pinched soon after, and these days, with the licence not having to be renewed each year, well . . .'

'They asked about burglars and visitors to the house and she told them she had none except her friend in the flat downstairs, also a widow, and she had never been burgled.'

'Wonder who sorted the old man's stuff?'

George Binns consulted the notes he was holding. 'Her sister, also a widow.' He grinned ruefully. 'Came down from the north and helped but according to this there wasn't much because they had got it down to a minimum when they moved to that flat a couple of years before.'

'Not much there then, but someone got hold of that licence somehow. You know, George, it's the little details that snooker you. If it wasn't stolen in a break-in it could have been in a wallet or a coat that was given to a jumble sale, for instance. Right, someone buys this coat or wallet, finds the licence and chucks it away in a dustbin — no, that's no good, it would have been shredded to pieces or burnt. Let's try again. It's in a coat pocket — a lot of men keep their driving licence in the inside pocket. Right, our buyer of the jumble sale coat or suit goes to put his own wallet or whatever in the inside pocket as he walks down his path. He unzips it and feels this other item there, pulls it out, looks at it as he walks down the road, and throws it into the first public waste bin he sees.'

'And our bogus Mr Welsh comes along and takes it out in case it should prove useful later.'

'Something like that, George. These things turn on a hundred-to-one chance. The type that regularly rummages through waste bins must occasionally turn up something important. If our character was a shady one anyway he would certainly hang on to something like a current driving licence.'

'So he keeps it, and after he's murdered Arnold Brand, Betty Morse learns who he is and he has to silence her. He uses Peter Welsh's driving licence to hire a car and stage Betty's 'accident'.'

'Too much chance, isn't there, George? The other thing is a connection between Arnold Brand and Mrs Welsh. What is to stop her from hiring someone to murder Brand for her, and when Betty became a nuisance, giving the hired man her husband's licence . . . '

'That is presuming Brand had something to do with Gloria Welsh's suicide, chief.'

'Yes. But the flaw there is that so long elapsed between the two incidents. Nevertheless, I think we'll keep our eye on Mrs Welsh, George. I can't ask for a watch on such flimsy guesswork — we'll play a waiting game.'

'Did you go to the play last night, chief?'

'Yes, I did. Listened very carefully to their voices — pity there isn't a Scottish character in the play, but our man is too canny to have picked an accent we could check on simply by going to the theatre. Didn't think much of the play, to be truthful, George, but maybe that's because I know they're all tensed up about other things.'

A smile hovered round Sergeant Binns'

215

mouth but he kept silent. He knew his boss enjoyed opera and Shakespeare so could imagine his frustration at having to spend the evening watching and listening to these people he had been quizzing all day.

'As to the clerk's description of the hirer, I think Prince Kingly is too short to fit our bogus Peter Welsh, although with his background he's likely to be a bit wild. He could have been wearing built-up shoes which would have made him much taller. Or he could have had someone else do the dirty work for him, of course, but that would be risky.'

'Roger Johnson is about the right height and build, so is Tim Merry and most of the stagehands. Charlie Ferguson is too tall. Then again it could be someone from outside. Rob, Iris's boyfriend, fits the bill — maybe too fair and flamboyant, though, but he could have worn a wig. He's an actor and any tricks of the trade would probably go unnoticed in a normal situation like hiring a car.'

'Especially by such an unobservant assistant as the one in that garage, chief! Who else is there on our list?'

'Tom Holman, but I think he'd be more noticeable. He doesn't quite fit the description anyway, and let's face it, Arnold Brand was such a bastard he probably had everyone he'd ever worked with wanting to kill him. I've been studying the report on the gun too. It's possibly an old wartime one — a Luger — which makes me wonder again about the Welshes. That could have gone missing about the same time as the licence, couldn't it?'

'Shall I check?'

'Yes, George. One of us may pay another surprise visit to Mrs Welsh later, but see if you can get Paddington to check on whether her late husband brought a souvenir home from the last war, and if he did, where it is now.'

When his sergeant had gone from the office, John Carding walked over to the window once more. There was less activity below now; a couple of police cars parked and a constable striding across the forecourt.

'There's something I've missed,' he said to himself. 'Some connecting bridge I haven't paid enough attention to.' He reached up and opened the top of his window before telephoning the hospital to see how Betty Morse was. No change, he thought gloomily at the end of the brief call. And apparently no-one had been to the hospital to try to see her. In a way this was a relief to him, yet if just one of them had been there it would have given him a reason to delve further into their motive. A picture of the understudy Peter

Strong came into his mind. Now he *had* asked the inspector how Betty was and if she needed anything. When he told him she was still in a coma and no visitors were allowed yet he muttered his thanks and turned abruptly away. He hadn't requested permission to visit, though — just asked if there was anything she required.

★ ★ ★

Charlie Ferguson, the stage doorman at the Victoriana, was making a model theatre for his granddaughter when John Carding telephoned.

'I have to be out your way around lunchtime today, Charlie,' he said. 'Any chance of a chat in your local?'

They arranged to meet in the Royal Oak, a few minutes' walk from Charlie's cottage, at 12.30.

Sitting at a table in the corner of the snug, Charlie took a pleasurable swallow of his ale. 'Best bitter for miles around,' he said. 'How can I help, Inspector?'

John Carding picked up his glass of orange juice. 'I agree about the beer but I can't indulge while I'm on duty. Now, how you can help? To tell the truth, I'm not sure. Nothing specific but you can fill me in on any visitors, fans, locals or otherwise who have come to the stage door since the season started.'

'A tall order, sir.' Charlie grinned. 'In a holiday town like Fairbourne there's different faces each week. Yes, a lot of locals also come — there's an elderly woman who's as regular as clockwork. Always appears at the stage door after the show to have a word with the cast of whatever play is on. But . . . ' He pursed his lips. 'I can't recall anyone behaving strangely.'

'I didn't expect there to be, of course. Our murderer isn't likely to draw attention to himself in a way that can easily be traced afterwards. How about the company, Charlie. Noticed any odd behaviour there?'

'They're *all* pretty tense — naturally enough, I suppose.' He shook his head. 'Nothing really, though, and I have been watching. Can't help myself, I s'pose — old habits die hard, sir. Of course there wasn't anyone hanging about by the stage door after the matinee on *that* day. It's the evening they wait to see them mostly. Pity, really, because if anyone *had* tried to get out while I was investigating Crystal's screaming, there'd have been a witness.'

'Well, go on keeping your eyes open. By the way, did you know Jack Hawkley at your last station?'

'The police surgeon. Yes, sir. Good chap.'

'Friend of mine. Was best man at my wedding.'

★ ★ ★

Inspector Carding returned to the station in time to take a call from Paddington police.

'Grace here. A quick return on your query about Mrs Welsh. One of my men was going to that area this morning and he called. She vaguely remembered her husband bringing home a revolver and a camera from the war, but she didn't know the make, type or anything about them, and said she had no idea where either of them were now. Sergeant Boyce, who called, said she denied her husband brought anything at first, but when he suggested a captured gun and jogged her memory a bit, she thought he had, and then she recalled the camera, but she was sure they weren't in the flat.'

'Thanks, Inspector.'

'Not a great deal of help, I'm afraid.'

'It all adds up to a complete picture eventually,' Carding said, with more confidence than he felt. He pressed the buzzer for Sergeant Binns. 'Got a job for you, George,' he said. 'I want to know how many of the company at the Victoriana own cameras

— cast, technicians, stagehands, even old Bill the odd-job man.'

'Right, chief.'

'Wait. Not a direct question. I want it casual, during conversation. Mrs Welsh says her husband brought a gun and a camera back from the war. Presumably it was a German camera. Find out if any of them own a German camera, circa 1945. You can invent a police photographic competition if you like, but keep it conversational. An off-duty policeman talking about his hobby. I'm going to see Iris Brand now. It's not a matinee day, is it?'

George shook his head. 'No. Wednesdays and Saturdays are matinee days.'

At the door he turned, as he often did with his interviewees. 'George.'

'Sir.'

The inspector grinned. 'Good luck.'

* * *

The sun was shining and Sloane Avenue was quiet — a haven of peace. No children tearing up and down on bicycles or radios blaring out loud and unmelodious music. A gracious part of the town to live in, Inspector Carding thought, as he pulled up in front of the Brands' house.

It was a few minutes before Iris Brand answered the door, and he gazed around the well-ordered front garden and contemplated how much a house in this avenue would cost. She didn't open the door wide, only enough to see who was there.

'Mrs Brand — Inspector Carding,' he said. 'I apologize for coming unexpectedly, but if I might have a word. I won't take up much of your time.'

'Of course, Inspector. Come in, please.'

He followed her into the comfortable room he had been in on the last visit.

'Will you have some coffee, Inspector? There's some bubbling.'

'Well, in that case, thank you.' While she was gone he wandered round the room. Good furnishings, and a Chinese carpet that must have cost my wages for a year, he thought. There weren't many photographs — one beauty of Iris on stage in a crinoline, another of her by the railings on the promenade on a stormy day. He paused to look closer; a happy one, that, her hair windswept and she laughing into the camera lens. There were two more — an elderly couple in a garden, probably her mother and father, and a tiny snapshot in a heart-shaped silver frame, of Robert Mantle. That certainly hadn't been there last time. Not one of her late husband anywhere in the room.

'There, didn't take long,' she said, returning with a tray. 'Oh, do please sit down and make yourself comfortable, Inspector.'

Was it his imagination or did she seem more relaxed, more confident than before? Or was she simply acting a part — hostess to the man tracking down her husband's murderer?

He put a spoonful of brown sugar into his coffee and said casually, 'Just been looking at your photographs.' He indicated the snapshot of her in the storm. 'That's very good — you can almost feel the spray. May I ask who took it?'

A closed look came over her face but she answered him quietly. 'Rob Mantle.'

'End of March if I'm not mistaken,' he said. 'It was a bit rough then, I remember. He's got a knack with a camera for sure. Is it a good one?'

She shrugged. 'I don't know. Why?'

'No particular reason. I'm interested in photography, that's all. Now what I really came to talk about was your late husband. I know I asked you before, but sometimes when one has had time to think about it, other memories return. His enemies, Mrs Brand — can you think of anyone who had a reason to hate him enough to murder?'

She seemed to lose both colour and

confidence and return to the quiet, even frightened woman again.

'No,' she said after a moment.

'Did you know your husband was in fact blackmailing several people?'

She looked straight at him then, her eyes pools of silver and grey, with reflected depths he hadn't noticed before.

'No,' she said, 'I didn't, but I'm not surprised. He was every kind of an evil man.'

'Go on.'

'I'd rather not, Inspector.'

'Whatever you tell me will go no further than this room, Mrs Brand, unless it absolutely needs to. On the other hand, what you tell me could lead to catching your husband's murderer.'

His eyes never left the actress's face and after a few moments she looked downwards.

'You do realize that you are one of the main suspects, Mrs Brand?'

Without looking up, yet every word distinguishable, she said, 'He preyed on young girls. Turned on the charm and after a few months, sometimes only weeks, he tired of them. I was only sixteen when it happened to me. My parents made him marry me because I became pregnant.' With a catch in her voice she said, 'I lost the baby at seven months and I couldn't have any more. He

224

never forgave me. He was brutal. Later, after one or two close shaves, he turned to older women.'

'Yet you never left him?'

'He wouldn't contemplate divorce and he would have found me if I had just gone. We lived separate lives in the same house. I directed all my love and energies into my career from then on and we often didn't see each other for months at a time. He was secretive about his affairs.'

'I understand and I'm sorry to ask you to go through this but it is vital to our enquiries.'

She looked up. 'He wanted to be a star, top of the bill, and he did make enemies trying to do this.'

'Was he jealous of your standing in the theatre, Mrs Brand?'

'Yes.' Her voice was a trembling whisper in the quiet room. 'And he made me pay for it. He was a vicious man, Inspector, and I won't pretend to you that I'm glad he is no longer here. I often wished I had the nerve to kill him myself.' She stopped suddenly and, looking him squarely in the face and her voice becoming stronger now, she said, 'I didn't kill him but I can't mourn him either.'

19

Two days later Sergeant Binns had checked all the suspects' cameras. 'Except, of course, the German one that has been hidden purposely if the camera and the driving licence were stolen together,' he said to Inspector Carding.

The inspector paced up and down his office. 'I had a worrying thought when I was shaving this morning, George, and I believe we could be on completely the wrong track. Arnold Brand may not have been murdered to stop the blackmail at all. That may have been a sideline for him and somewhere out there is the real reason he was murdered.'

George waited while his boss did another turn round the floor.

'I don't know yet what the motive was, but let's ignore the blackmail and start again with an open mind. He wasn't extorting hundreds and thousands of pounds out of anyone — in fact, he was rather clever in his approach to his victims, George, because he never asked for more than they could afford, and I suspect he never pursued it once they were apart.'

'I can see what you're getting at, chief. But then it opens the net wider.'

'Not necessarily. One of our suspects here in Fairbourne could have done it. Someone who had a grudge against him for something else. Apart from those he was blackmailing, who stood to gain from his death?'

He walked back to behind his desk and sat down, pulling a large pad towards him. 'Let's take the cast and workforce of the Victoriana first,' he said.

Twenty minutes later he had covered six foolscap sheets with his spidery written remarks. This was John Carding's off the cuff way, when a case was defying all the official avenues. This was his way of synchronizing his thoughts — he needed to get them on to paper but not in an official manner. In the writing down of his feelings, even so briefly, sometimes something gelled.

Sergeant Binns stood quietly by, and eventually his chief looked up and said, 'Well, sit down George, it won't cost you anything.'

George Binns grinned. 'If it was not one of the cast or staff at the Victoriana, then we have to acknowledge that whoever did it had inside help.'

'Yes, I think you're right, George. And the easiest but most unlikely person to help them would be Charlie Ferguson, stage-doorman and ex-policeman. He is genuine ex-police. I tested him with an old pal in the force. But let's face it, there are bent coppers. I'd be sorry if it was that,' he added.

'What about Roger? They shared the dressing room.'

'Unknown quantity. No obvious motive, but a connection with Betty Morse before their working stint down here.'

The two men were used to working like this — during their years in the force they had done so over many mysteries, and when working in London some years ago over two murders. Sergeant Binns never doubted that his chief would solve the case; he just hoped he could solve it quickly before anyone else got hurt.

'So really we're back to square one,' Sergeant Binns said. 'The most likely person, or persons, to have murdered Arnold Brand are within the cast or stage personnel of the Victoriana theatre.'

'It seems so,' the inspector said carefully. 'Robert Mantle had a motive, but he also has a pretty watertight alibi. You can't always spot the guilty quickly, but you often can the innocent, even when they confuse the issue with their own cover-ups. I wish I knew more about Gloria Welsh though. It seems too long a time but I've a suspicion there's a connection, if only I could trace it.'

He drummed his fingers on the desk. 'The obvious one is that Brand was blackmailing her about the baby, but if someone was going to knock him off for that, they'd surely not have left it five years?'

'You don't think it's chance that the hit-and-run driver used Peter Welsh's driving licence? That it was among the loot he'd got from somewhere?'

'No, George, I don't. Too much of a long shot. Not impossible, but not probable. Now if Mrs Welsh paid someone to kill Brand — and I would not have thought she'd have the kind of money a hitman would demand — then why did she wait five years?'

'Maybe she suddenly came into some money. Perhaps she *had* to wait all those years to afford it.'

'But she didn't seem . . . ' he hesitated ' . . . bitter, did she? Unless she's a very good actress herself.'

'I think she was genuinely surprised when you asked her about Gloria, chief. Which means that if she is uninvolved, we look outside for the killer. For someone who planned the murder meticulously, no fingerprints, no sound, and, if it's someone we've already grilled, a rigged alibi!'

'But not as clever as he thought if Betty

Morse stumbled on something, which I'm convinced she did. That was no ordinary hit-and-run job.'

'What's the latest on Betty?' George Binns asked. 'Because if our man is still here and she recovers, she is in even greater danger.'

'The situation doesn't look good. She's in a deep coma. Right, introspective session over, George. I've got to see the super in half an hour.'

When the inspector had left, Sergeant Binns went into the front of the station.

'Not sure if I want promotion — if you're an inspector you get all the flack,' he said to the desk sergeant.

'No further news on the Victoriana murder then, Sarge?'

George shook his head. 'Nothing yet but the governor'll do it if he's given enough time. Any tea going?'

There was and he took the tea into the office and set to on a stack of paperwork that had built up on the desk.

Meanwhile John Carding strode purposefully along the corridor upstairs to the superintendent's office. There were two strands to this case, he thought. One the blackmail angle and one a completely different reason for someone to kill the actor. The common knowledge part was that a lot of people, his enemies amongst them, knew he was in a play in Fairbourne and with a bit of research could have found out which was his dressing room and when he was likely to be in there. If Brand wasn't murdered because of his blackmailing activities, a closer look at his life was needed.

Iris Brand's voice echoed in his head: 'He preyed on young girls,' she had said. An angry and devastated father, someone completely outside the world of the theatre, he thought, or even a grandfather if it involved a beloved granddaughter.

Why did he feel in his bones that somehow, somewhere along the line, Gloria Welsh, a young woman who had been dead for five years, who died by her own hand, was mixed up in this murder? The fact that Arnold Brand had been in the cast of a play all that time ago wasn't anything to go on by itself, but the hit-and-run driver with the hired car and a driving licence in the name of Peter Welsh was pushing the margins closer. There had to be a connection. He just hoped the super would give him enough time to fathom it out.

He had cut his original lists of suspects in half because their alibis checked out perfectly. Unless two people were involved and one was covering for the other but he didn't think that likely. Roger Johnson was in the clear unless he had bribed the waitress in the cafe opposite the theatre. The murdered man's widow, Iris, was on stage at a theatre in Eastbourne and her lover performing in Worthing.

Peter Strong, the understudy, had the opportunity because he was supposed to be off sick that day and they only had his word for it. So far no motive had emerged for him and he was, after all, the one who saved Betty Morse from going to the bottom of the cliff.

Inspector Carding was standing outside the superintendent's office now and, clearing his mind of these present thoughts, he knocked on the door.

20

Inspector Carding was in the bath when the idea hit him. He set his mind to focus on the scene in the dressing room where Arnold Brand was killed. The man was wearing underpants only. His shirt was on a hanger on the rail and his tie was hanging over the mirror. Hold on — was it his tie? Two men shared that dressing room and Roger wasn't likely to go round to the little cafe he often frequented with his collar and tie on, or was he?

Lathering himself vigorously, he pictured the scene. Roger coming in and divesting himself of his stage clothes in favour of something more casual before going for tea and cake. Of them all, Roger Johnson had the best opportunity because they shared the room. But where was the motive? So far they had uncovered nothing that would suggest he was a blackmail victim like some of the others. They may not even have been in the room together. If Roger was there first it would only have taken minutes to change and vice versa, he thought. But Arnold wasn't changing so much as stripping and if Betty's stories of Roger Johnson being very puritanical were accurate then he probably didn't approve of what went on with Crystal and was very glad to be out of the way as fast as possible. In his statement at the beginning of this inquiry he said Arnold was not in the dressing room when he went in to change. 'I was no more than a few minutes and he hadn't arrived before I left, but that was normal. Occasionally we were in there together, but not often. We did tend to keep out of each other's way off stage. Sexual orgies are definitely not my scene.'

Carding turned the hot tap on and let in more water, while his imagination played around with various scenarios for those minutes when someone shot the actor. It was meticulously planned right down to a gun with a silencer. Whoever it was didn't even need to be a brilliant shot because the deed was done at close range. It would take a good marksman to hit someone in the right spot from a distance with a gun fitted with a silencer, he thought, because they were inclined to make the weapon top heavy. But in this case anyone relatively inexperienced with a gun could be successful. It didn't rule out expert Tom Holman, of course, who had at least two reasons for wanting the man out of his life and was also used to handling guns.

He could have been in the room already and would possibly be familiar with the layout backstage. Perhaps he hid in Crystal's dressing room for a while and escaped through the stage door in those moments when Charlie was engaged in Arnold and Roger's room. A brisk walk along the road to the car park and he'd soon be back home without anyone knowing where he had been, or even that he'd been out at all.

John Carding luxuriated in the water a few moments longer, then climbed out of the bath and towelled himself dry. Nothing like a relaxing bath to ease tensions as well as aching limbs, he thought. As he pulled on his pyjamas trousers, deciding it was too hot for the top, his mind moved to Prince Kingly. There was the blackmail and the fact that Kingly had a record of violence — but it was a long time ago and he had been clean for many years. By his own admission he was in the theatre when Brand was shot, but then so were several of the actors and the lighting man. The stagehands had both gone out between shows. Would Kingly have planned the shooting so well, though? He struck Carding as much more of a spur-of-the-moment man and George Binns' analysis of his handwriting bore this theory out. Nevertheless, Prince Kingly was a serious contender. You couldn't rule anybody out in an inquiry like this.

Then there were the girls. Betty was in the clear unless she had murdered Arnold and the clifftop and speeding car were true accidents. But a hit-and-run driver who had hired a car under a false name — a name which had cropped up in a five-year-old suicide case — seemed ominous. And Carding didn't believe in too many coincidences.

He padded downstairs in his slippers and walked into the sitting room. 'I'm off to bed now, Ruth. Do you want a drink before I go up?'

'No, I'm fine, thanks, darling. I won't be long myself. Once I've got to the armhole — ' she indicated the knitting in her hand ' — then I'll call it a day.'

John locked and bolted the front and back doors and, taking a glass of water with him, returned to the bedroom. His body may have been relaxed but his mind was racing still. He thought about Nicola. Bit of an unknown quantity and what was it George had deduced from his studies? 'Control and attention to detail.' He recalled the sergeant's exact words: 'exceptional control, very strong-minded.' Yet she was another one who didn't appear to have been blackmailed. Maybe she had resisted, he thought, and Brand was putting the pressure on. Must find out if she knows anything about guns or if she owns or has access to them.

He was up to assessing Iris, the dead man's widow, when Ruth came to bed.

'Still awake? I bet I know what you've been thinking about,' she said.

'You'd likely be right too, but I'm switching off now you're here, my love.'

★   ★   ★

The next day, after a few routine tasks, John Carding went to see Tim Merry. He called on the off chance because he didn't want to make the man more jittery than he already was, and he knew he would get a better result if Merry hadn't had time to think about it first. Contradictory man, he thought: a nervous worrier and a martinet at the same time. No wonder he seemed to have a permanent headache. He was in the wrong job if he wanted a smooth and peaceful ride.

Tim was at home and it was obvious from his expression that he thought the inspector had called to tell him that the murderer had been captured. Carding shook his head and came straight to the point. 'May I see the script of the play you were doing the day

Arnold Brand was killed, please, Mr Merry?'

'Yes, of course, Inspector. Come in and I'll find it for you.' He led him into a small and tidy sitting room. 'Wife's out shopping. Make yourself comfortable and I'll fetch it. Should be in my office.' Carding looked around him. There were photos of children in various stages of growing up around the walls, and one of a beautiful young woman dressed in a long gown. She was on a stage with a line of dancers behind her. He walked over and studied it for a few moments but was back in the chair when Tim returned, clutching a sheaf of scripts. He thumbed through them. 'Here it is. *The Swapping Party*.'

'Thanks. Mind if I borrow it for a few hours? Something I want to check.' He stood up, then pointing to the picture of the young lady and the dancers he said, 'Beautiful girl. Who is she? It looks like the Tiller Girls behind her.'

Tim smiled properly, about the first time John Carding had seen him not looking as if the end of the world was imminent, as he told Sergeant Binns later.

'It *is* the Tiller Girls and that — ' he walked over to the photograph and said with unmistakable pride in his voice ' — that is my wife.'

'She is stunning.' Carding tried to hide the

surprise he felt. 'A dancer then?'

'Yes. If she had gone to Hollywood, Ginger Rogers would have needed to watch out. A singer too — she has a lovely voice. She sang with Richard Tauber once at a special concert for charity but she gave up show business when we started a family. Says she's never regretted it but I sometimes wonder.' Abruptly he turned from the picture. 'She is still involved, though. Now the children are older she helps with many dancing troupes in and around this area and she choreographs for one of her friend's productions. That's how she met Nicola.'

The inspector looked at him steadily. 'Nicola Coates?'

Tim's worried look was back. 'Yes, that's right. She was in a variety show a couple of years ago which Edna was choreographing and they hit it off and became friends.'

'I thought Nicola had worked in a circus?'

'She did. She was a sharpshooter but she could sing and dance too and she had this ambition to act. But I mustn't keep you, Inspector. I just hope we can soon see an end to this awful business.'

'Don't worry, we will. It's all part of our job,' Carding said. 'Tell me more about Nicola, Tim.'

'I don't know any more. She's not a bad

239

actress but dreadful at learning her lines. I've had one or two run-ins with her, but I have to be tough with them all or we'd never get the show off the ground. It's not easy managing this lot, Inspector.'

Carding moved towards the door. 'Well, thanks for these.' He rippled the papers in his hand. 'I won't keep them long and I will look after them.' He had the strange thought that he didn't want to be responsible for putting even more lines on the director's craggy face by pursuing his questioning.

★ ★ ★

'It struck me that Tim Merry wanted us to know Nicola was a crack shot, George,' he said to his sergeant later. 'And I gave him the opportunity by commenting on that photograph. Food for thought, though. She told me she had been in a circus with the horses mostly, but she never mentioned her speciality.'

'Probably thought we might jump to the wrong conclusion, guv.'

'Mmm. I think Tim is worried because he realizes she hasn't told us. Methinks our Miss Coates is a girl of many talents, George. Some more delving into her background is necessary — what other secrets is she keeping from us that the late unlamented Arnold sussed out, I wonder?'

★ ★ ★

He talked to Nicola later that day. 'Exactly what did you do in the circus, Miss Coates? I'm not too clear about it.'

'I worked with the horses,' she said, 'but I always fancied myself as an actress or dancer.' Before Carding could say anything she went on in a rush, 'I do find it difficult as an actress. It's not proving a great success so far,' she added. 'Remembering all the plays, and rehearsing one and acting in the other. It takes a lot of concentration and I think I'm probably a do-one-thing-at-a-time girl.'

John Carding said softly, 'What did you do with the horses?'

'I was a bareback rider.'

'And?' he prompted.

'Did stunts. You know, a somersault as we went round, that sort of thing.'

'Does that sort of thing include sharp-shooting?'

There was barely a pause before she said, 'Sometimes, if the performer is a good shot and trained for it.'

'And you qualified under both of those criteria, I believe?'

Nicola lowered her gaze and he saw that she was trembling and her face had gone quite pale.

'Come now, Miss Coates. Your main job with the horses was as a sharpshooter. You rode round the ring, hitting a moving target, isn't that right?'

He wasn't anything like prepared for what happened next. The girl opened her mouth to answer him and then slumped downwards in her chair. Rushing forward, he just saved her from crashing to the floor.

★ ★ ★

When Nicola opened her eyes again she was in a hospital bed and a white-coated doctor was advancing on her with a syringe in his hand. She screamed and suddenly she was being held down by strong capable hands and a woman's voice said, 'She's back with us, Doctor.'

The syringe moved away and the doctor said, 'That was quite a scare you gave us. How are you feeling now? Better?'

'I wouldn't have done it,' Nicola said. 'I could never have killed him, no matter what. I loved him too much.'

The doctor and sister inside the curtained-off area with her looked at each other and the doctor mouthed something to Sister Field-mark.

'Who couldn't you have killed?' she said gently.

The answer when it came was almost a whisper. 'Jimmy. It was an idle threat, but he thought I meant it. He was halfway across when I came in to practise. I would never have done it, I swear I wouldn't. I didn't know he was there.'

'What was he halfway across, my dear?'

'The tightrope, of course. And he didn't have the safety net down. Only for the performance because it was the rules. Oh, he was such a daredevil.' Her voice sounded strange, as though it were coming from a distance, and every so often it got caught in a strangled sort of sound as though she was choking.

'I was riding Benjy and I didn't look up there but I had the gun in my hand . . . Suddenly he was falling. Oh God!' She covered her face with her hands and wept.

Great heartrending sobs shook her tiny frame and Sister Fieldmark's arms went round the girl as she said gently, 'Tell me about it and I can help you.' As the doctor moved silently away, the story of Jimmy's infidelity and her threat to kill him unfolded. How she had ridden in astride her horse,

Benjy, ready to practise shooting, which she did at some part of every day. 'I'd set the targets moving and I didn't see him above me on the rope. He always worked in the morning and I did mine in the afternoon, but that day he came in the afternoon. I didn't shoot but as I looked up he saw me, missed his footing and dropped like a stone.'

Sister Fieldmark held the girl's hands as the tears racked her again. 'But you weren't to blame for his death,' she said. 'It was an accident.'

In the sudden silence, Nicola uttered three words. Her voice sounded almost unearthly. 'He didn't die,' she said.

★ ★ ★

John Carding got the story from Sister Fieldmark herself a few hours later when the patient was sleeping. 'Apparently Jimmy's injuries were life-threatening but he was young and strong and he pulled through,' he told George Binns. 'He lost a leg, had spinal injuries and will have to spend the rest of his life in a wheelchair. Nicola wanted to look after him but he refused to see her, and now his mind is going too. She poured her heart out to Sister Fieldmark apparently; they couldn't stop her talking about it once she started. She'd had it bottled up inside her for years.'

'Nicola Coates — yes, that's the control I saw in her writing. It was so strong. I suppose she blotted it all out and was able to function normally, but it was there beneath everything all the while.'

'That's about it, George. It's uncanny how you picked up on that. Well, uncanny to me, I suppose, but to you . . . '

'It's a guide, guv. And it had nothing to do with Arnold's death, did it?'

'We don't know, George, do we? The state she was in makes me wonder. She just went to pieces when I questioned her about the sharpshooting act. If Brand had found out anything about her story and was blackmailing her — well, she was an expert with a gun, she was one of the first on the scene when Crystal screamed, and she knew the time to do it. On circumstantial evidence, she's definitely in the running.'

'Yes,' George agreed. 'When did all this happen? The circus stuff, guv?'

'Several years ago. Nicola never returned to the circus. According to Sister Fieldmark the girl sold Benjy — she said she was in a terrible state when she talked about selling the horse — and simply left.'

'Presumably she then took up acting to earn her living?'

'Yes. She could dance, sing, was acrobatic and had no trouble getting into variety shows, but of course way down on the bill. She told the good sister all of this; I think she purged herself in that hospital today. No wonder she's sleeping now. If Arnold had found out her story and was blackmailing her I don't think she would have had any compunction in shooting him. He was nothing to her, not like the fickle Jimmy whom she loved. I feel sorry for Tim Merry,' he added. 'When I told him Nicola was in hospital he looked stricken. He has had more than his fair share of bad luck with this little lot.'

'Do you reckon he has his suspicions regarding Nicola, sir?'

'I'm not at all sure, but I do think it worried him that we didn't know about her prowess with guns. It does put a different face on the enquiry. It gives Nicola Coates a strong motive.'

21

'I don't deserve you, Edna, but I do love you so very much. I know I don't say it nearly often enough but it's true. I love you even more now than when we married and I didn't think that was possible.'

His wife picked up the cup of tea he had just brought to her and smiled mischievously at him.

'It's not just because of what you are doing to save our skins now, my dear, it's all the time.' He laid his hand on her shoulder and she reached up and patted it gently.

'I know, Tim, but you'd do the same for me if the boot was on the other foot. It's our good fortune that I have a sort of photographic memory so it's not as arduous as all that.' She glanced down at the script lying on the table in front of her. 'I can cope with it so don't worry, and Nicola will be back before long, I'm sure. Give me another half hour then you can test me on it,' she added. Planting a kiss on her shining brown hair, he did as she asked and moved away.

Edna Merry had suggested the idea of her playing Nicola's role until the girl was back from hospital. 'I've got all the right cards, Equity et cetera,' she said, 'so it will be perfectly legal and I don't think it will be for long anyway. It isn't as though Nicola has any physical injuries and the mental and emotional ones will possibly heal better if she is back in the fray. She will need the money too — that's a powerful pusher to get back to normal.'

Although she sounded so sure when talking to her husband, Edna privately thought it might be longer than the few days she had told Tim was likely initially. She had been to the hospital to see the girl and had been shocked by her pallor and languidness. When they had been in the variety show together Nicola was supremely confident in her general manner, yet now she looked and sounded extremely insecure about everything. She seemed to have distanced herself from real life, Edna thought. She'd not even asked how the show was managing with three cast members now missing.

Just as she was leaving, however, Nicola had reached out her hand. 'I didn't do it, Edna,' she said tremulously. 'I didn't kill Arnold. We argued, he was always putting me down and saying I couldn't act, and we did have words that afternoon, but I didn't shoot him. I don't even own a gun now.'

'I don't believe anyone thinks you did, Nicola.'

'The police do,' the girl said as she sank back on to the pillows. She closed her eyes then and as visiting was over and there was a general exodus through the door, Edna, with one backward glance towards the sleeping, or pretending to sleep, Nicola, joined the throng out of the rarefied hospital air and back into the hubbub of life outside.

She knew that Nicola had no close relatives, just a distant cousin living up north whom she very occasionally saw. Both her parents were dead, killed together in an accident when she was fifteen. She had been born into circus life and until she left and went into the variety theatre she had moved around the country with what she referred to as her 'circus family'.

She had not known the real reason Nicola had changed her lifestyle, although she guessed it was because of a man, but she had befriended the girl and encouraged her to go ahead with her acting career.

She was relieved at how Tim was coping with these latest setbacks. People often thought him weak but she knew that when he was up against it, something kicked in and he rose to the occasion. She never doubted he would, but she knew he could make himself ill doing so. In a way his worrying was a defence mechanism and it did get a little out of hand sometimes, but he would weather this little lot, she was sure, and as she would be right there in the theatre with him until Nicola was able to return, she knew he would draw strength from the knowledge. When a friend said only the other day, 'Your Tim's in the wrong job, Edna. With his worrying nature and this awful murder and illness at the Victoriana, well, it's not going to do him any good, is it?' she had said, 'Tim is stronger than most people realize. He'll cope.'

★ ★ ★

Inspector Carding took the clerk from the car hire firm in Eastbourne to the play the following evening, hoping he would recognize the now obviously bogus Mr Welsh. He didn't. The man couldn't pick out anyone on stage resembling the man who hired the car which ran Betty Morse down.

'I didn't take a lot of notice of his appearance,' he said. 'The licence was in order and he signed the form without any fuss. There was nothing odd about the transaction at all.'

'And there is no-one you've seen here this evening who sounds like him? Think. An inflection, a hint of an accent, anything, however slight.'

'I told you sir, no. And I'd be horrified if I picked the wrong man.'

'Don't worry about that. The police check thoroughly and no-one would be charged without proof.'

'I really don't recognize anyone Inspector.' He fidgeted and was obviously itching to get away.

'Of course,' John Carding said to his wife later, 'he didn't know he was being asked to pick out a murderer. He thinks it was a driver who didn't stop after an accident. And let's face it, our man obviously disguised himself even if unobtrusively. I mean, with his shoes built up even Prince Kingly, who is actually the shortest among the men, would match any of the others in the theatre.'

The latest news from the hospital about Betty was that she was holding her own. Miraculously she had no broken bones, and no really bad head injuries, but she did have internal injuries as well as bruising and cuts all over her. 'It's been known for patients to be in a coma for months and months, so it has,' Sister told John Carding, 'but on the plus side is the fact that often some of their injuries heal during that time. There's a lot to be said for letting nature take its course, so

there is. If she comes out of the coma . . . '
She looked him straight in the face. 'It's really
for the doctors to say, Inspector, but myself, I
think she'll have a fighting chance now of
pulling through.'

Peter Strong, the man who had saved her
on the cliff, had taken to calling at the
hospital each day to check on her progress.
He was barred from the ward — only her
family and the police were allowed to go in
and see her. This was an order from Inspector
Carding, who impressed on Sister the
importance of not allowing any of her staff to
admit anybody, no matter what reason they
gave for wishing to see the injured woman.
He had talked to her and the matron of the
hospital, enlisting their help to keep Betty
safe. 'We are dealing with a potential
murderer here,' he told them both. 'Someone
who might try to charm his or her way in.
This is, of course, in strict confidence.'

'No-one will get past my nurses, Inspector.
I promise you that.' Sister's Irish accent
sounded more pronounced when she was
being earnest and John Carding felt reas-
sured.

Betty was still in a small side ward close to
Sister's office and opposite the tiny kitchen
the nurses used for making tea and putting
patients' flowers in water. And there was a

member of the police outside her door during afternoon and evening visiting times.

'There is always someone responsible near her,' Matron informed him, 'and one of the nurses, or Sister herself, admits people to the main ward at visiting time. Anyone wishing to see patients in the two separate rooms has to check with her first.'

Double reassurance, he thought. The murderer seemed to be having it all their own way so far, but Carding knew the net was closing in. Unless it was someone from another area of Arnold Brand's life — and he had not ruled that possibility out, even though his gut feeling told him it was closer to home than that — then he had all his suspects under one roof. Whoever it was could not escape without giving the game away and they knew then they would certainly be caught. Carding's force had checked on home addresses, siblings, even more distant relatives and friends and had a comprehensive file now on most of the personnel at the Victoriana theatre. Someone had to stick it out until the end of the season or be judged guilty. Those who were innocent had nothing to worry about. They must be looking at each other and wondering, he thought. Betty was safe all the while she remained in hospital, and especially while she was in a coma. He was still convinced she had seen or heard something which told her who the murderer was, but of course she may not recall that when, and if — because it still was an if — she woke again. That was when she would need a safe house.

22

John Carding had a tidy mind, which is why he often caught criminals on the smallest change in their stories. He had asked them all what time they left their lodgings and what route and mode of transport they had used on the day of Betty's accident. Perhaps it was time to check this with them and see if they remembered what they had told him. The truth often varied by a tiny amount. People were seldom exactly precise in all the things they recalled.

He had his notebook, which contained their actual words on the day it happened and even a brief description of their individual reaction to the news. Shock registered in all the faces and in much of the body language, but he hadn't detected giveaway guilt. This murderer was a cool customer, if indeed it was someone within the company — and his strongest leads still suggested that it was.

Looking at his notes, he saw that Charlie had been at the theatre by 1.30 and begun checking the previous day's racing results, his mug of tea beside him as he waited for the cast to arrive. Tim had cycled from his home and was in the theatre by 1.45. Peter had been the first of the actors to arrive 'around' 1.50 or 1.55, according to Charlie. He had been closely followed by Nicola and Roger, who came in together, presumably having met outside. The couple of stagehands had already been there. Iris Brand's boyfriend Robert had been in Worthing and was a bit later than usual but was in his theatre there by 2.10 and Crystal had breezed into the Victoriana 'looking hot and bothered', Charlie had said, eight or nine minutes before curtain up.

John Carding saw that she had said she was late because 'I went to collect an item of jewellery I had left for repair at the jewellers near Burton's, the men's outfitters. The teddy boys who are always by the railings near there were so abusive to me that I went back inside the shop for a few moments and then asked if I could leave by the back door.'

When questioned further, she told him she was eventually allowed to do so, but this brought her into Wallace Street, from which she had much further to go, working her way round several small roads to emerge on the other side of Oliver's Memorial without having to 'brave the teddy boys' again. She had been hesitant over the form the abuse took, he had noted in his book, but eventually said they taunted her for being 'Brand's fancy piece' and suggested she had 'knocked him off' because he became too demanding.

Wrong way round, Carding thought as he recalled everyone else's interpretation of the liaison.

Crystal had, typically, burst into tears when telling him about the incident and said it was the reason she so seldom went into the centre of town alone. 'They used to simply wolf-whistle but when that local reporter wrote about Arnold, and about me being the one to find him, he insinuated so much that wasn't true . . . '

Her account this time round was much the same, except for the fact that she elaborated on the teddy boys' remarks and turned the episode into her own mini-drama, he thought. Yet basically it was the same story.

Sergeant Binns had visited the jeweller, who verified that 'the young lady had indeed been upset by the ribald remarks she had encountered' and they had allowed her to exit the back way.

Nicola, he noted, said she met Roger as she crossed over from the promenade where she had been 'taking a breath of sea air before going to work'. As she was now in hospital he couldn't check her statement this evening. Roger's had tied in with it.

'I spent part of the morning in the library, told my landlady I was going for a walk over the hills in the afternoon and hoped to get as far as Bolford then catch the bus back and would probably go straight to the theatre, so she very kindly gave me a packed lunch.' He said he saw Nicola crossing the road from near the pier and they walked the last few yards to the Victoriana together.

Prince Kingly had spent the day in Eastbourne with his current girlfriend. 'We walked up to Beachy Head, had some lunch, then back down to the town and the beach but it was pretty crowded, so we got the bus back to Fairbourne, went for a swim, then into my beach hut for a while before I came back to my digs to change before the show.'

He could not check on many of them but those he could verify proved to be true. Roger's landlady had packed him some sandwiches that morning and had done this before because he did often go walking across the hills during the daytime.

Once clear of his digs, however, he could have gone anywhere. The same applied to Kingly. He had said he didn't know where his girlfriend lived because he had only met her the day before on the beach and they had rowed after they returned from Eastbourne to the beach hut in Fairbourne and he hadn't seen her since.

'Her name?' Inspector Carding asked quietly.

No hesitation there, anyway. 'Sonia. I don't know her surname.'

'Does she work in Fairbourne?'

'No idea, Inspector. Work was not what we talked about.'

That left Iris Brand and Tom Holman. Their stories tallied with what they had previously said. That didn't make them true, Carding thought, but for the moment he had to believe they were where they said they were at the time. Tom *could* have been the driver, but Iris would have had to have a male accomplice. Both had reasons for Arnold Brand to be eliminated from their lives.

He toyed with the idea of Tom Holman first. It would have been easy enough for him to do some research on Betty's time and route without anyone knowing. The chap from the garage could have been right when he said he didn't recognize the bogus 'Mr Welsh' on stage the night he took him to the play.

Then again, he reasoned, Iris could have hired a hitman to kill Arnold. She had the kind of money for it and her husband's death left the way clear for her and Robert Mantle.

If Betty Morse had somehow discovered this, the same man could have been at the wheel of the white car which ran over her. His gut feelings rejected this idea immediately, yet he had to consider it.

★ ★ ★

Tom Holman was as cross as ever at being disturbed. 'I have already told you I was at my desk the entire afternoon. Mrs Mac, our housekeeper, brought me a plate of sandwiches around noon before she left, and I saw no-one until Crystal came in later that evening and told me one of the cast had been knocked down by a car which was travelling much too fast.'

'She mentioned the speed of the car?' John Carding questioned.

'Yes, Inspector, she did, but I would think by now that even you would have deducted that my wife has a dramatic nature. She would be incapable of stating a simple fact without embellishing it. Now, if you will excuse me, I have work to do.'

Iris Brand quietly reiterated that she was in Eastbourne, sitting on a seat on the front and enjoying the sea breeze.

'You were not with Robert Mantle?'

'No, Inspector.'

'Why?' His voice was gentle but he watched her reaction extra closely this time round.

'He was in Worthing with another performance to do in the evening and I was in the same position in Eastbourne. Both of us had two performances that day. We are in love, Inspector, but we don't spend all our time together.' Her smile softened her words.

★ ★ ★

'So that's about it, George,' Carding said to Sergeant Binns. 'There are no real discrepancies in the stories this time round from last time. Of course, we have to remember we are dealing with a group of people who are very used to rehearsing and remembering.'

23

Inspector Carding wandered into the Cafe Bertini, which was diagonally across the road from the stage door of the Victoriana. In spite of its Italian-sounding name, it couldn't look more English. Red and white gingham tablecloths, small vases of fresh flowers, and a very faint but appetizing whiff of toast issuing from somewhere behind the tall counter. It was three o'clock in the afternoon and there were a few people in there. Most of them had drinks and a cake in front of them, one or two something more substantial like baked beans or egg on toast.

He chose a table halfway down the aisle and looked around him. On the walls were black and white photographs of film and stage stars: Greer Garson, Betty Grable, Veronica Lake, Humphrey Bogart in a scene with Lauren Bacall, Clark Gable, James Cagney and his own especial favourite, a beautiful shot of dark-haired Margaret Lockwood in a scene with James Mason from *The Wicked Lady*.

A pert-looking waitress came over to his table and he picked up the menu and studied it. 'I'll have a cup of tea without sugar and a toasted teacake, please.' Indicating the pictures around them he said, 'Wonderful set of stills you have here. Being so close to the theatre, I daresay the actors and actresses from there come in frequently. None of those up here though.'

She gave him a cheeky grin. 'Different class of actor. These are all stars, *proper* stars. That lot over there are just ordinary people really. Oh, some of them are quite good, but you can't believe in them like you can these.'

'Do you go and see the plays on your night off?'

She looked at him coquettishly and he suddenly realized that she thought he was trying to chat her up. Embarrassed, he said quickly, 'I know one or two of them slightly and they said you could always get a good cup of tea in here.'

'Do you? Did you know the one that was murdered?' Her blue eyes sparkled.

'Er, no, I didn't know him personally. Was he one of your customers?'

'No, never saw him. Bit spooky though, in't it? An' no-one's been arrested so there's a murderer at large in the town.'

There was a mixture of adventure and fear in her voice, then she looked closer at him as though trying to assess if he could be the wanted man. He had purposely dressed casually for this little excursion so that he could talk to the staff in an unofficial capacity.

A man appeared behind the counter and the girl busied herself with a little notepad and pencil, which were hanging from a band of ribbon tied to her belt. 'A toasted teacake was it, sir? Anything with it?'

'No, that will be fine, thank you.'

When she had gone he looked around him. The couple in the corner by the window seemed engrossed only in each other, while the other window table was occupied by a middle-aged man and woman who had the distinct look of holidaymakers.

In a surprisingly short time the waitress was back with his tea. 'Food will only be a few moments,' she trilled. 'Are you on holiday or do you live here?' The flirting look was back and Carding wondered if this was the waitress Roger had taken on a couple of dates. He was sorry now that he had come in here incognito because he could hardly return as a policeman to question her later — it would look odd. George had spoken to the girl Roger had been out with before, probably this one, so he would have to let him do the official questioning again. When the teacake arrived he ate it slowly, wondering if she would return and volunteer any further information. Just then there was a sudden influx of people, a holiday group by the look of it, and he knew he had mangled his opportunity completely. Damn, he thought, as he wiped his mouth and pushed back his chair. The girl was there in a flash with his bill. He paid and left a generous tip. 'I hope we shall see you again, sir,' she said before hurrying over to the table by the window.

★ ★ ★

'Got a pleasant little job for you, George,' he said when he was back at the station.

'What's that then, guv?'

'Go and talk to the waitress or waitresses at Bertini's, that little cafe near the Victoriana. From one of the window seats there you could watch who went in and out of the stage door of the theatre. If you'd a mind to,' he added.

'Am I looking for anything specific?' the sergeant asked.

'Yes, as a matter of fact you are. I want to know which members of the cast at the Victoriana frequented the place regularly, how many staff they have, and especially what they wore.'

He turned to look at some papers on his

desk and George, looking slightly puzzled, said, 'What they wore? What the actors and actresses wore, sir?'

'Yes. Particularly on the night of the murder.'

'Right.'

'And George?'

The sergeant turned to face his superior. 'Yes, sir?'

'Especially Roger and Prince. We know Roger dated one of the waitresses on a couple of occasions, not sure about Prince. Would think he went for slightly more glamour. The one in there is quite homely, nice girl, but, well, as I say, homely, if you see what I mean. Not exactly Prince Kingly's type, I wouldn't have thought. She may not be the only waitress, of course.'

George had worked with John Carding long enough to know there was more to come so he stood silently and waited. Sure enough, after a few seconds the inspector said, 'I — er — was in there myself earlier this afternoon but I bloody well botched the job. Went incognito and the wretched girl obviously thought I was chatting her up.'

George Binns' face remained still, not a muscle moved, and Carding went on, 'I think that tie over the mirror in the dressing room was Roger Johnson's, not Arnold Brand's. Find out what shirt or top he was wearing when he was there that day. I've got the script of the play they were doing when Brand was killed so we can check on the clothes they came off stage in.'

★ ★ ★

Sergeant Binns in his official capacity wasn't a great deal more successful than his inspector, but he enjoyed a strong cup of tea and one of his favourite Chelsea buns. He ascertained that Lorraine, the young waitress, was the only one. 'His nibs' wife comes in on my day off,' she confided.

Lorraine couldn't remember what sort of clothes Roger Johnson was wearing that fateful day. 'He had some trousers on,' she said, giggling into her hands. 'I'd 'ave noticed if he hadn't, but I didn't see what colour they were.'

'Jeans, grey flannels, light or dark?'

'I told you I don't remember. I'm too busy here most of the time to notice what the customers are wearing. Run off me feet, I am, sometimes.'

★ ★ ★

'Didn't even know if he had a shirt or loose top on, whether he was wearing a jacket or cardigan or pullover. I checked shoes or sandals as you suggested, but no-go. She looks at faces not feet, she informed me rather sharply. A most unobservant young lady,' George reported back.

'What about the date they made?'

'For the tea dance on the pier on Sunday afternoon apparently.'

'And did he keep it?'

'Yes. She said he was a good dancer and he mentioned that they must do it again. He walked her home but wouldn't go in — said he had to check over his part in next week's play ready for the Monday morning rehearsal.'

'More likely he didn't want to get involved by meeting the family. It seems he likes to play the field.'

'Right. And the young lady, she's called Lorraine, said he wasn't wearing a tie on the Wednesday but he was when they went to the tea dance on the Sunday. 'Real smart he looked, an you could 'ave used his shoes as a mirror to powder yer face, you could, they were that shiny.'' George did an imitation of the girl's high-pitched voice.

John Carding laughed. 'Not bad, not bad at all.'

He stood up and walked round the desk. 'Roger Johnson shared the dressing room so he'd have the best opportunity, George. Agreed?'

'Agreed, guv.'

'But any of them could have slipped in before Crystal got there and no-one, except the victim, would have been any the wiser.'

'Agreed again, guv.'

'So, if we presume for the moment that it is one of the theatre people, then Crystal is another obvious choice. For opportunity, I mean.'

'Mmm. But he wasn't blackmailing Roger or Crystal as far as we know, was he?'

'No but he might have been. We simply haven't discovered the reason yet. Another thing, George — if Betty hadn't gone along to Crystal's room and made her later than usual our murderer still had plenty of time. As it happened she did delay Crystal for about fifteen minutes or so and that gave the perpetrator time to organize his story. Or her story, as the case may be. What I'm getting at is they had a chance to get themselves together so to speak and we mustn't forget that this bunch are all in the acting profession and that must make it easier for them to fool us all if they set their minds to it.'

Inspector Carding had looked through the script for *The Swapping Party* and found that in the final scene the men were all in lounge suits and the girls in cocktail-length dresses. 'Five minutes or so to change, wouldn't you think, George? After all, they would have a routine.'

'That sounds about right. Brand was in the throes of doing so when he was shot. He had his trousers and shirt and shoes off and got it right in the middle of that lurid tattoo. Was he in the navy during the war? Sailors often get themselves tattooed, don't they?'

'Yes, but he was too young for the war — he did his national service in the army though. Could as easily be someone from those days. Reckon he ferreted out a lot of unsavoury things in those two years, but it's harder to trace. If we could find the reason, we'd have our murderer. How about Prince Kingly — did he frequent the cafe?'

'Sometimes, but although he flirted with her, I gathered they had not been out together. 'He's a card that one,' she said, 'but he's a bit short for me. I like a man to have to stoop ever so slightly to kiss me good night.'' He didn't tell his boss the last bit of that conversation when she had added, 'Like you'd have to, Sergeant.'

24

It was Thursday again, changeover day, and as usual tempers were frayed. They had a rehearsal in the morning and Tim found himself praying everything would go well for the evening performance. That no-one would forget their words or suddenly come out with a line from the current play, or that any of the other disasters he frequently dreamed of would happen. Last night he had dreamt that the grandfather clock fell on to the back of the settee and tumbled on to Crystal and Roger, crushing them as they sat down. At the point of impact Tim jumped, and Edna, startled out of her sleep, reached over to him. His body was drenched with sweat.

Tim was always anxious before a first night but this season had been the worst yet. The police hadn't caught Arnold's murderer and everyone was jumpy. At first it seemed that everyone had presumed an outsider had got in and shot the actor. He himself thought and desperately hoped this was the case, but now the cast were beginning to be seriously suspicious of each other. It was more obvious at rehearsals than at the performances when they were on show to the public; behind the scenes the atmosphere was quite different. His own thoughts see-sawed between believing it *must* have been someone from outside who killed Arnold and the niggly doubt that it was an inside job. He could barely think about that, but with no further news from the police he knew they were all under suspicion. After all, anyone from a stagehand to one of the cast would have had an opportunity to kill him far easier than someone who came into the theatre illegally.

Then there was the business of the gun in Crystal's dressing room. Inspector Carding said it was a plant and not to worry about it, but that was impossible for him, and probably for Crystal too. Being sworn to secrecy over the incident didn't help. He had imagined that would only be for a day or two at the most but the ban on talking about it was still in force now and it weighed heavier on him each day.

He and Crystal had not mentioned it to each other since it was found, although he did wonder if she had told her husband, Tom. There were so many questions in his mind. Why, if she hadn't killed Arnold herself, was the gun in her dressing room? Someone hid it there. Was it because they wanted to throw suspicion on her, or was it because they were disturbed before they could get out and hid it in desperation? That would suggest they knew where to hide it but surely it would have the murderer's fingerprints on it?

Gloves. Of course, the final scene of the play they were doing that awful day was a wedding scene and all the ladies wore gloves. But the killer, whether man or woman, probably did too. A long and deep sigh escaped from his lips. He must stop these thoughts. Already he could feel something like a band of steel tightening in his head and he had tonight's performance to get through yet.

★   ★   ★

The two stagehands brought the furniture needed for the entire play from the shed and left it in the yard while they relocked the building. Swiftly they carried the bookcase with its mock-up books on to the stage, then the large table for the dinner party and the six velvet-lined dining chairs. The chairs were quite worn, but under the lights they looked good. Next was the small sideboard, which they placed beneath the window that looked out on to the 'garden'. Finally a silver tray complete with glasses. A decanter of sherry, some bottles of authentic-looking wine, and a bottle opener which they arranged on the chest. The taller of the two men placed a vase of make-believe flowers on a round lace mat in the centre of the highly polished table. Then they left.

★ ★ ★

With thirty-five minutes to go now to curtain up, Charlie arrived and ensconced himself in his cubbyhole with his thermos flask of tea and the evening paper. No one else was likely to get here for another ten minutes or so. He unfolded the paper and began to read about Eden's victory in the general election the day before. It rehashed the facts that he had taken over when Churchill resigned in April but that this was his victory, and he was now an elected prime minister in his own right, with an overall majority of sixty. Decent majority too, Charlie thought. A real vote of confidence. His eyes scanned the results from the various constituencies but although he took a keen interest in politics and usually checked them all, tonight his heart wasn't in it. He laid the newspaper on the shelf behind him. Somehow this evening he simply couldn't concentrate properly — his mind kept returning to the night of Arnold Brand's murder, and not for the first time since then he meticulously ran through as much of the preceding period as he could recall. Something might pop into his mind that would give a clue to this murder business, he thought.

Because it had been a matinee day he hadn't gone home between shows. Never seemed worth it — it would be different if he lived round the corner, but he was a good twenty-five minute walk away. After the matinee he had settled himself comfortably on his cushion on the high stool with the back to it which he had originally brought from home. He always had something to eat between shows on matinee days and on that Wednesday it was cheese sandwiches. He clearly remembered saying to Jean how good it was now rationing had finally finished and how he relished being able to have thick slices of his favourite cheddar and they had laughed about it together. Everything had seemed normal. The cast arrived at their usual time — apart from those who hadn't left the theatre between the matinee and the evening show. This was usually Crystal and Arnold, and sometimes Nicola, who stayed to make a fuss of Vicky, but all the others went out for an hour. Doris actually asked if he wanted anything brought in as she was popping to the shop. 'A roll or a cake or something?' she suggested, and he reached for the sandwiches his wife had made for him and waved them at her. 'My favourite tonight,' he said. No, there was nothing wildly different. Everything and everybody had seemed normal until Crystal's scream rent the air.

He was catapulted back to the present as the cast started to arrive. Doris was last. She dashed in ten minutes before curtain up. 'Got held up with one of my neighbour's children,' she said breathlessly. 'Thought I'd have to bring her with me but luckily her mum arrived just before we left.' Doris had a small part as a maid in this play as well as doing Betty's role. She came on towards the end of the first act when Crystal and Peter Strong (in their respective characters) had wandered hand in hand through the door and out of sight into the garden. Doris's job was to collect the glasses they had been drinking from and begin to set the table for the dinner party, grumbling about the family and the extra work while she did so. As part of the action of the play, she only ever got as far as putting on the tablecloth when a demented ex-lover rushed in, brandishing a gun and shouting, 'I know they're here, they won't escape me this time,' and crashing through the door leading into the garden. There is an almighty bang and the curtain comes down.

The beautiful cream damask tablecloth was kept in the top drawer of the chest and Doris always checked that it was there before the play began. She hurried through and quickly pulled open the drawer. It was there, but scrunched up as though there was something hiding beneath it. A fleeting thought went through her mind that a bird or some small animal had somehow been trapped in the drawer and she gently picked up the bundle and opened the edges of the cloth. She just managed to stifle a scream — because she knew the audience were the other side of the curtain — and her face drained of its natural colour as she saw the revolver in her hand. Laying it carefully back in the drawer, she raced backstage to find Tim Merry.

He phoned the police station. He had difficulty in getting the words out when John Carding came on the line.

'Is the audience in the theatre, Tim?'

'Yes, yes, it's curtain up in six minutes' time.'

'Not tonight it isn't. Don't start or touch anything until I arrive,' Carding instructed. 'I'll be with you very quickly.'

'But — '

'No buts about it, Tim. Keep those curtains closed and everything just as it is. I'm on my way.'

It was ten minutes later when he arrived in the theatre and the audience were growing restless.

He demanded the tablecloth the gun was concealed in. It was Doris who pointed out that it had since been ironed and folded neatly and was again residing in the drawer of the chest ready for her to take out and set on the table. A furious inspector took the gun, wrapped it in a special cloth he had brought with him, and returned to the police station.

'I'll be back shortly,' he said to Tim. He heard the slow hand-clapping from the audience as he went out. When he reached the stage door, Charlie was drinking a beaker of tea. 'I am now co-opting you, Charlie Ferguson,' he told him. 'Detain anyone, cast, stagehands, electricians, *anyone* at all who tries to leave the theatre.'

Charlie stood up, 'Yes sir,' he said.

Back at the station John Carding handed the gun to forensics. 'Though what you'll find there probably won't be any use,' he remarked. 'I fully expect our murderer to have wiped it clean before leaving it there, and within the last half hour it has had at least half a dozen people handling it. And they even ironed the bloody tablecloth and put it back in the drawer. That's probably on stage now being contaminated by the rest of them.'

'But you've got the gun, sir, and now know it has to be one of them for it to be where it was.' George always called his boss 'sir' when things were going as wrong as this.

'Hmm. Was pretty certain of that before.' He paused. 'What time are you off?'

'Ten o'clock, sir.'

'Right. Meet me at the Victoriana in half an hour. Interval should be on then. We can talk to some of them.'

★ ★ ★

Tim Merry wasn't the only one who thought the questioning should be left until the play was over and Carding said, 'You have a choice, Mr Merry. Either I talk to them during the interval or we drop the curtain now and send the audience home. Which is it to be?'

Of course, word had got around backstage that the gun that killed Arnold Brand had been found. The two most perplexed people were Tim and Crystal. Tim had queried it earlier, and Carding admitted that when tested the one in Crystal's dressing room was not the weapon that killed him. Crystal could scarcely believe that another gun had been

279

found and was more jittery than ever before. Because of limited time if the show was to continue after the interval, the cast and the stagehands and electrician who also operated the lights were gathered together in Tim's small office to hear Inspector Carding say, 'We have found the gun which killed your colleague, so things will start moving now. Has anyone here anything they wish to say? If you have seen or heard something unusual, something different from the normal let us know, either now or privately afterwards so we can check it out. It doesn't matter if you think it isn't important, or even that you haven't mentioned it before. It could be that final piece in the jigsaw that clears this case up and I'm sure that is what you all want.' There were uneasy murmurings from those present, a bit of shuffling of feet, but no one spoke.

'Right then. I shall be here for the rest of the evening should you wish to see me. You all know where the police station is and I can be contacted there any time.'

He moved towards the door, opened it and quietly went out, leaving a very stunned crew behind him. He had Sergeant Binns and another detective posted at front and back of the theatre and had reinforced his instructions to Charlie. The two police officers knew this. John Carding then stood in the wings watching the action, and especially the body language of the actors and actresses on the stage. If the murderer tries to break out, all exits are covered and if he or she realizes the police still haven't any strong evidence and brazens it out they will have to do so for another three or four months at least, he thought. Anyone leaving the show after tonight, on whatever pretext, or however genuine they made it appear, would surely be admitting their guilt.

25

Inspector Carding looked solemn as he handed Sergeant Binns a wad of papers. 'Go through these if you get time this morning, will you, George?'

The sergeant knew his chief was worried. He had been on edge from the time he touched down rather earlier than usual that morning.

'The latest news on Betty Morse is that she is holding her own,' he said, 'and the other item is that Nicola Coates is being released from hospital today. Tim Merry's wife, Edna, is going to collect her and apparently she is returning to work this evening.'

'That should take one worry line from Mr Merry's face,' George replied.

'You're right there. The atmosphere at the theatre is very tense now. Let's hope the girl can cope with it. That strength and determination you saw in her writing should help.' He went through to his office, dealt with a few routine matters that needed his attention and then sent for Sergeant Binns again.

'George, I'm going to see Mrs Welsh. I

don't believe that driving licence was stolen — I think someone in the family has it, or at least has had it recently. It could be a relative. We know she has a sister, the one who helped her clear up when her husband died. She could have brothers and uncles and if she herself was not involved in that hit and run, one of them could be. And the only reason for that has to be the connection between the murdered man and the Welshes. If Brand was milking the family dry about Gloria's baby, a dedicated and united family could have decided to eliminate him to protect the girl's name. And of course to save money as well. I'm going to find out if any of her family have links within the theatre world.'

'Right, sir.'

'We need more about Gloria's background, although at eighteen she didn't have time to create much history. If anything vital comes to light I'll be calling on Detective Inspector Grace at Paddington — you can contact me there.'

John Carding left the building and walked to the railway station. On the train he closed his eyes and let the cast and theatre personnel of *The Swapping Party* roam through his mind. Sometimes something struck a cord — a word, an expression, something intangible that didn't fit in with the known facts.

Nothing specific, yet something was out of place. That might have been how Betty knew, for he was convinced now that she did. Stumbled on the odd thing out and realized . . . which meant the killer was still in Fairbourne, probably within the theatre circle.

He called into Paddington Police Station before going to see Mrs Welsh. Inspector Grace was out so he said he would look in later. Then he walked through the hot streets to Mrs Welsh's flat. When there was no reply he tried one of the other bells, and within minutes the door opened a fraction of an inch and the round, pink-cheeked face he had seen on his last visit peered through the chink.

'Good afternoon,' he said, 'I am sorry to trouble you. Mrs Welsh seems to be out — do you know what time she will be home, please? I need to speak to her urgently.'

'No.' The woman looked startled. 'I've no idea at all.' Before he could expound further she closed the door and he heard a bolt being drawn. Well, he didn't blame her, but he had a thought he might learn something about Gloria's mother to fill in the time. He walked away down the street, certain that the bubbly-faced lady was watching from her window.

He spun out a cup of coffee in the cafe on

Paddington Station, and then returned to try to contact Mrs Welsh, whom he suspected was in her flat all the time anyway. He was anxious not to startle the woman but determined to follow this niggly feeling which kept cropping up whenever the hard facts ran out. He could be wildly off course and the driving licence and Betty's accident have nothing to do with Arnold Brand's murder, but he didn't think so. Although he dealt in solid facts nine tenths of the time, he trusted his instinct for the other tenth. If it was right it would lead to the facts and the truth. It was usually right.

She answered the door herself this time, almost as though she had been downstairs waiting for him. Probably didn't want the other tenants to see the police going in, although he wasn't uniformed. Her reluctance to see him was natural, he thought, given that he was reviving a sad and difficult time in her life, but he could tell she didn't like to refuse to talk to him — she was of the generation who had a healthy respect for the police.

'If I could have five minutes of your time,' he said, 'just to check a couple of small points about that driving licence. I won't detain you for long.' He smiled to himself at his police language, which he knew often amused and sometimes exasperated his sergeant.

He had begun this jaunt with high hopes but now they had faded. If Mrs Peter Welsh was involved with Arnold Brand's murder she wasn't going to give herself away, and when it really came down to it, he had not a shred of evidence about her. The fact that her late husband's driving licence had been used to secure a hired car which had knocked down Betty Morse might have no bearing on the case, but his policeman's logic and mistrust of coincidence made him think otherwise.

He followed her upstairs as he had on that other occasion, but this time she took him into the sitting room, which had been undergoing decoration on his last visit.

'You said it was about my late husband's driving licence, Inspector. Well, I told the policeman from our local station all about that. I simply do not know what happened to it.'

'I understand your sister helped you to sort things out?'

'That's right. It could have been thrown out with the rubbish — after all, it wasn't of use to anyone except Peter. I was naturally rather upset at the time, and Dora didn't worry me with things that didn't matter. Why is it so important?'

'If it fell into the hands of an unscrupulous

286

person,' he said, watching her reaction, 'a person who wanted to hide his own identity, the only name we would have to check him by would be your late husband's.'

'But how could it fall into anyone else's hands, Inspector? If it was with Peter's stuff, nobody here would be able to use it anyway.'

He smiled at her naivety and, turning away from her, gazed round the cosy little room. It was then he saw the photographs. One of a glamorous young girl in an evening gown, the other a head and shoulder portrait of a young man. They were on the sideboard and there was no mistaking that lean, scholarly face and those thoughtful-looking eyes. It was a several years younger version of Roger Johnson.

In his excitement he stood up, startling her. 'It's all right,' he said, 'but I've just noticed that photograph and I recognize the face. He's an actor in the play currently on at the Victoriana theatre in Fairbourne.'

'That's right,' she said. 'That's my son Roger.'

'Roger Johnson,' he said. 'A stage name?'

'No. He's my son by my first marriage.'

'Ah. When did you last hear from him, Mrs Welsh?'

'What, hear from Roger?' She sounded startled at the turn the conversation had taken. 'He sends me a postcard every week but he doesn't come home often because he's usually away touring. In any case he has his own flat near Victoria station. He did pop in one Sunday last month though; he had to come up for something in the flat, he said. It was a lovely surprise. He's a good son, keeps in touch regularly, especially since my husband died.'

Suddenly she clutched his arm. 'He's all right, isn't he? Nothing's happened to him? He's not been in an accident, has he?'

A fleeting spasm of compassion for this woman shot through John Carding's body, but he said calmly, 'No, he's well and working hard.' He walked towards the door.

'Is that all?' she said. 'Did you come all this way to ask me exactly the same questions as the other one from Paddington Station?'

'I was up here about something different,' he lied comfortably, 'and decided to see you while I was in the vicinity. I'll see myself out,' he added. 'And thank you, Mrs Welsh.' She stood, small and defiant, looking up at him. 'Roger hasn't got his father's licence,' she said. 'He has one of his own, so he doesn't need to pretend. He's been driving since he was seventeen.'

'Did he get on well with his stepsister Gloria, Mrs Welsh?'

'Oh yes. He was devastated when she died.

We all were, but it was a long time ago. We learned to cope with the shame.'

'Shame?'

'The baby.' She was whispering now. 'Gloria was going to have a child — it came out at the inquest. You checked on that. I could tell you knew the last time you came here.'

'Yes, we did. It's part of our job,' he said, 'to sometimes probe into other people's distress, but if it doesn't help our enquiries then it goes no further, I do assure you.' He closed the door quietly, feeling guilty about the unshed tears in her eyes, and as he hurried round to the police station he imagined her looking sadly at her daughter's picture on the sideboard and remembering.

Inspector Grace was in and he produced train timetables and from there Carding telephoned Sergeant Binns in Fairbourne.

'George, listen. Get round to the Victoriana and stay there until I get back. Unobtrusively — don't be on display. Roger Johnson is Peter Welsh's stepson — and Gloria Welsh's step-brother. I'll be there before the curtain descends tonight — meanwhile keep a discreet eye on Johnson. He mustn't suspect what we know.'

'OK, chief.'

'And George?'

'Yes, sir.'

'I want a constable posted outside the the-atre, back and front, but not too obviously.' Detective Inspector Carding looked at his watch. 'And have a car meet the 7.15 from Victoria. Due in at Fairbourne at 9.31. I'll be on it.'

★   ★   ★

John Carding felt the excitement rising from the pit of his stomach as he made his way on the packed underground from Paddington to Victoria. He had a meal on the train, which was crowded with commuters, and he thought how fortunate he was to live and work in such a pleasant town as Fairbourne. True, this murder had been a nasty business, and it wasn't finished yet because he had still to make a case against Roger Johnson. Circumstantial evidence alone may not be enough to convict him but he knew now that he was the killer. He had killed Arnold Brand because the man had blackmailed his beloved stepsister, Gloria. But he had covered his tracks well, and John Carding had to prove his case.

He had probably thrown Peter Welsh's driving licence into the sea or burnt it by now. No, his trump card would be the surprise because Johnson must be thinking he was getting away with it. He wasn't a fool — he knew the police would keep the file open and that the entire cast would be on the suspect list, but when the season finished he would go away from Fairbourne and probably never accept another engagement within miles of the place. Most likely change his name — so they had to nail him now. John felt exalted. Half the battle was knowing who was guilty.

He told the constable who met him with a car to take him back to the police station. From there he telephoned his wife. 'Ruth, I'm afraid I'll be late again tonight, darling, so don't wait up. It could be a long vigil.'

Then he went to the theatre. Charlie was in his usual cubby-hole at the stage door. 'Sergeant Binns said to tell you he's in Bertini's cafe over there,' he said quietly, and at that moment George himself appeared in the doorway.

'Saw you arrive, sir.'

'Play finishes in half an hour,' George said.

'That's fine. Is Tim Merry in his office, Charlie?' he asked.

'Yes, sir. Shall I tell him you're on your way?'

'No, thanks, I'll just arrive.' He looked across to his sergeant. 'Have you rung your wife? It could be a late do.'

'Yes, chief.'

'OK. Let the play run to the end and get the audience out as fast as possible, and then I want to talk to everyone again. I'll make the arrangements with Mr Merry now. I want all the exits from the auditorium locked or blocked once the people have left. That includes the toilets.' He looked at Charlie. 'No-one is to leave the building, and I mean no-one, whatever excuse may be given. Can you arrange that?'

'Yes, sir.' Charlie almost saluted.

26

As the curtain came down for the final time, Inspector Carding and Tim Merry walked on stage. Both wings were covered by young police constables.

'Something must have broken for the inspector to be here this time of night,' Prince Kingly said to Nicola, who was standing beside him in the line-up.

She looked round, saw the solid form of John Carding and stumbled. Prince's arm quickly shot out to support her and he could see goose-pimples appearing even through her makeup. 'It's all right,' he whispered. 'Just another grilling, I expect.' Standing upright now, she pulled away from him and ran for the wings. When she saw the policeman blocking the way she dashed back, leapt from the stage into the auditorium and raced up the centre aisle.

Roger Johnson sprang instantly into action. 'Don't worry, I'll get her,' he shouted as he too took a flying jump from the stage to go after her.

'No panic, all the exits are covered,' the inspector said to Tim Merry, who was standing next to him looking like a theatre ghost. Sergeant Binns glanced at the drop from stage to ground, then went through the wings and down the steps into the stalls to go after them. He was no athlete and wanted to get home to his wife later without any broken limbs.

Nicola was running through the rows of tipped-up seats in a desperate attempt to shake her pursuers off. Roger was close behind her now, his long legs catching her up easily, and for a few madcap minutes she zigzagged her way through and back into the aisle as George Binns, running to the end of the row, spread his arms wide and caught her full on. 'It's all right,' he said quietly, 'nothing bad is going to happen to you.' She began to sob and with his arm gripping her tightly, he led her back to the stage where the rest of the cast were watching the mini-drama with varying expressions of amazement, horror and even excitement on their faces. Doris came forward and put her arms round the trembling girl. 'It's all right, my pet, I'll look after you,' she soothed.

Roger too had returned. He shrugged his shoulders as he joined the group on stage, all still in their costumes from the final wedding scene of the play. With a nonchalant movement he reached up and took off his top hat. 'Well, obviously you won't be needing us now, Inspector, so can we get out of these togs?'

'Not yet. There are some questions I want to ask you all before you leave the theatre tonight. As you are being so helpful I'll begin with you, Mr Johnson. The rest of you may go to your dressing rooms until I send for you.'

Roger stood perfectly still, Sergeant Binns so close to him their arms were touching, while John Carding ushered the others past the constable in the wings. The only movement came from Johnson's eyes, which flashed from one side of the place to the other, his gaze sweeping swiftly from top to bottom of both stage and auditorium. They sat in two of the chairs so recently occupied by the wedding guests in the play. Roger looked tired and John Carding said, 'We won't keep you long, Mr Welsh.'

His startled look contained, fleetingly, fear and relief. But he was a cool customer, the inspector thought, when he said, 'Welsh? No, my name's not Welsh. It's Johnson.'

'Sorry. Of course. I got confused because I was talking to your mother today — to Mrs Welsh, that is.'

He couldn't hide the anxiety now, and he leapt from the chair to be swiftly and firmly pressed into it again by Sergeant Binns.

'What did you say to her? You didn't upset her, did you?'

'Of course not, Mr Johnson. We only asked her a few questions. She was quite happy about it.'

'Oh my God.'

'She doesn't know about Arnold Brand, does she? You may as well tell me the whole story, because I know most of it anyway.'

Suddenly Roger was quiet — he stopped clenching his hands one against the other, although his knuckles were tense and looked almost transparent through his skin.

'What about Arnold Brand?' he said. 'I have an alibi for the time he was killed.'

'I know. We've talked to the waitress in the cafe. You made sure she'd remember you were there then because you asked her for a date for the Sunday tea dance, didn't you?'

'She's a pretty girl, and I'm not tied to anyone,' he snapped.

'How long does it take to kill a man, Mr Johnson? When you have the gun with you and you are sharing a room? A few seconds — a few silent seconds using a homemade muffler on the weapon. And who would take any notice of you leaving the room — your own dressing room? If anyone had seen you they knew you left the coast clear for Crystal Holman between the matinee and the evening performance. But you saw no-one but the cat, did you? And that animal ran in terror and hid because it knew with an uncanny extra sense that something terrible had just happened. I am taking you into custody. Please stand.'

Roger obeyed. He stood like a statue, no movement showing anywhere on his face or body. It was as if someone had waved a wand to immobilize every muscle.

'I charge you that between 5.15 and 6.15 on 12 April, you unlawfully killed Arnold Brand, contrary to common law. You are not obliged to say anything, but anything you do say will be taken down and may be used in evidence.'

Roger Johnson came back to normality slowly. Suddenly his face looked thinner than before, and his lips were drawn together in a tight line of pain, yet his eyes remained harsh as flint. Without raising his voice he said, 'If there's a murder you need a motive. I haven't got one. Couldn't stand the man, as I told you, but neither could anyone else here. You don't kill someone you don't like — that's far too drastic. You can't pin it on me.'

'Try this for size,' Inspector Carding said. 'Five years ago your stepsister committed suicide. At the inquest it emerged that she was pregnant — '

'The dirty bastard,' Johnson broke in. 'I vowed then I would get the man who did it if I ever caught up with him.' His face was alive now with a raw hatred which made John Carding shiver inside, but once started it was as though he couldn't stop talking. Words poured from him.

'I did too; I avenged my lovely little sister's death. I planned it carefully from the moment I was sure. I had my stepfather's old souvenir of the war — I found it in a pile of stuff Aunt Dora had put out for a charity shop to collect. And I was fond of the old man — he never made any distinction between me and Gloria when we were kids — so I took his gun and his camera as keepsakes. He'd taken them off a German soldier. When Gloria died I vowed vengeance on the man who did it — I didn't know how, but I would find a way. But for five years I've never known who it was. None of us did. The only thing she said in that hospital where they tried their damnedest to save her was 'Starfish'. My mother said she was wandering in her mind, but I knew it had to be a nickname.'

'How did you know Brand's was Starfish?'

'I didn't — not at first. But one day we were in the room together and he took his shirt off to change and I saw it. A huge starfish tattooed across his chest — and I knew. It was as much as I could do to stop myself strangling him there and then, but I'd had years to think about it — about what I should do when I finally met the beast. Because I always knew I should one day.'

Roger Johnson wasn't looking at them now and he seemed to be talking to himself, his voice very quiet and precise, yet hatred was oozing from every syllable.

'I checked that he was in *Lads and Lassies* with our Gloria and from the moment I was sure it was him I planned every move: an eye for an eye and a tooth for a tooth, the Bible says. I had our father's gun and I had until the end of the season so I could pick my time ... ' His lips came together in a harsh thin line and he nodded his head. 'As I fired I said. 'That's for Gloria, you brute.''

Tears were streaming down his shock-white face now and he seemed unaware of his audience, delivering his explanation as though he were saying lines from a play. It was as though he had to say it all now he had started.

Suddenly his mood changed and his voice became quiet. 'I hope Betty recovers. She saw me putting the prop gun in Crystal's room. That was the bit that went wrong and I was truly sorry to have to eliminate Betty, but I never meant to have to answer for that beast's death . . . '

'And why Crystal's room?' the inspector said softly.

'Because she's a bitch. Two-timing that husband of hers, and anyway she was the most obvious person to have killed him. Everyone knew she went to his room between the matinee and the evening show each week.'

John Carding said quietly, 'I think it's time to go.'

Sergeant Binns produced a pair of handcuffs from his pocket and Roger flinched. 'Please,' he said, 'do I have to? There will be people out there watching. I would like to walk out normally this last time.'

George looked at the inspector, who inclined his head in assent. Walking between them, his arms linked to each of theirs, he was like a zombie. They went past the constable still standing in the wings, then walked silently past Charlie and the constable guarding the stage door, and out into the street.

Then Roger Johnson broke away. They were holding his arms on each side, were almost by the car waiting in the kerb, when he thrust his elbows backwards with an almighty jerk and was off.

Carding and Binns chased him, dodging

the theatre-goers who had been waiting outside the stage door, and the many who parked their cars in that road behind the theatre.

With the two of them hot on his heels he dashed down a side street and into the main road. He had a long stride, was at least twenty years younger than either of them, and he ran with the spur of a hunted man.

I hope that driver's on to headquarters, Carding thought as he dodged the late evening holiday saunterers.

The police car pulled up beside them with a screech and the officers scrambled in. They wove in and out of traffic and on to the front, which was the direction Roger was heading. Carding contacted the police station and asked for a car and two men to get to the railway station quickly in case the wanted man doubled back and tried to get on a train. His eyes scanned the streets as he said, 'He's no money on him, he's straight from the performance, so he can't get far.'

'A boat,' Sergeant Binns said. 'He could go round into one of the little coves and hide until dark.' They were heading along by the esplanade now, and were almost up to the fishing quarter when they spotted him. He was no longer running but was walking fast and tagging on to groups of twos and threes as though he were actually with them.

'Keep him in sight. If he keeps on this path there's nowhere he can go when he reaches the end, unless he scales the cliffs,' Carding said. At that moment Roger, as if he sensed their presence, looked round, saw them and dashed across the road, causing the car in front to brake and the police driver to do the same. The inspector leapt out. 'Swing over and head him off coming back. I'll monitor him here. Send for another car to go up the cliff road, in case he takes the lift to the top,' were his final instructions as he dodged between the held-up vehicles in pursuit of his man. He reached the bottom of the lift in time to see Roger rush past the ticket booth and leap on as the doors were closing.

'Hey, you haven't paid!' the official shouted after him, but the mechanism had already begun and very slowly the cabin of the lift began the climb to the top of the cliff.

Carding hoped the police car he had asked for would be there in time. 'Can you prevent the doors from opening at the top?' he asked the ticket collector. 'There's a man wanted by the police in it.'

'Struth. Was that the bloke that got on without paying?'

'Yes. Can you do it?' The inspector's gaze travelled to the lift, which was even now a third of the way up the cliff face. 'Just long enough for us to get up there and arrest him. There's a car on the way.'

'Well, I'll be damned,' the man said, picking up a two-way phone to talk to his opposite number at the top. John Carding looked again at the lift slowly grinding its way to the summit. It was about halfway now and the one coming down was equal distance and as they passed some of the passengers waved to each other. It looked like a happy summer holiday evening, he thought grimly, but locked into that small space with six or seven others was a murderer who was now desperate.

Sergeant Binns materialized at his side. 'He's not in that lift, guv, is he?'

'Yes, he is. Is there a police car at the top?'

'They were all out but one was being sent ASAP, sir.'

'Come on, George, where's our driver?' Back in the police car, Carding barked out his orders. 'Top of the cliff, fast as you can.'

It was a winding road and they broke all the limits. The lift was already there but the door was closed and a great babble of noise was coming from the inside of it. When the operator saw the policemen he released the doors. Roger was so close to them he almost fell into the inspector's arms but thrashed his way out and began to run. George Binns came at him one way, the driver of the car another and Carding close behind. There had not even been time to handcuff him. His long legs galvanized into even greater speed by his urgency, Roger raced across the grass where a few holiday families letting their children have an extra late night grabbed them out of his path. Carding was one side a few feet behind him and Binns the other side, but the sergeant was closing in. There was no way he could go except forward towards the clifftop but he kept doggedly on. The space was clearer here, and Roger seemed to put on a final spurt.

George Binns had been the fastest in the class at his school, and had kept up the running even when he joined the police. He was in tiptop condition and now he was gaining on his quarry. Within touching distance and just inches from the edge, Roger stretched his arm behind him and grabbed the sergeant's hand, pulling him with him. Teetering on the very edge of the clifftop Sergeant Binns suddenly felt himself being pulled back and Inspector Carding's breathless voice panting, 'let him go, George, for Christ's sake let him go.'

As Roger Johnson disappeared over the clifftop, his scream echoed back to the two officers, who had tumbled backwards with the force of the tug of war. They scrambled to their feet and raced to the edge. Johnson was at the bottom, looking, in the moonlight and from this distance, like a small, flat drawing in the sand.

'Ambulance is on the way, sir,' the constable who had been driving them said quietly. As they approached their own car, Inspector Carding reached out and laid his hand on Sergeant Binns' arm for a couple of seconds, 'Don't you ever do that to me again. My God, I thought I'd lost you, George.'

★ ★ ★

The second telephone call the following morning sent Sergeant Binns hurriedly into his boss's office. 'It's Sister Murphy, chief. Betty Morse has opened her eyes.'

It was much later in the day, after talking to the sister and lifting the police ban on visitors that Sergeant Binns drove the inspector to the hospital. Peter Strong was already sitting by Betty's bedside. It was even later when they were sorting out their notes on the Victoriana murder.

'You know, George, right until the end, once I knew it was Johnson, I thought he had killed him because Brand was blackmailing

Gloria over the illegitimate child. Strangely, I didn't realize then that Brand was the father of Gloria's baby. Given her family background, she didn't dare go home in that state.'

'Roger adored his stepsister — he was twenty-four when she died, and she just eighteen. He vowed vengeance on the man who had sullied her, and that vengeance never died. During the five years which elapsed between Gloria's death and Roger's discovery of the man, it smouldered dangerously.'

'Can you imagine his feelings when he accidentally discovered that the actor he was sharing a dressing room with was Starfish, the only clue he possessed? From that moment, Arnold Brand was a marked man.'

'I take it his mother never suspected?'

'No. Poor soul. Roger never told her he had found Starfish. We're all strange mixtures, aren't we, George? I mean, take Roger Johnson, for instance. He had quite a way with the ladies himself. Nicola, Betty, Crystal, the girl in the cafe.'

'Do you think Betty Morse loved him, chief?'

'Love? What is love? I suppose Gloria Welsh loved Arnold Brand or thought she did or she would never have got herself into that situation — not with her background she wouldn't — and Roger adored her with a protectiveness that older brothers sometimes have for the pretty little stepsister who dotes on them. I hope it didn't go too deep with Betty — her feelings for Roger, I mean. She's a long enough haul ahead of her anyway now, poor girl. But she, unlike Gloria, has a compassionate family to help her.'

'And judging by the expression in his eyes when he looked at her in the hospital this afternoon, possibly the understudy too, eh, chief?'

John Carding laughed. 'Have you been reading Priscilla Chester, George?'

We do hope that you have enjoyed reading this large print book.

Did you know that all of our titles are available for purchase?

We publish a wide range of high quality large print books including:
Romances, Mysteries, Classics
General Fiction
Non Fiction and Westerns

Special interest titles available in large print are:
The Little Oxford Dictionary
Music Book
Song Book
Hymn Book
Service Book

Also available from us courtesy of Oxford University Press:
Young Readers' Dictionary
(large print edition)
Young Readers' Thesaurus
(large print edition)

For further information or a free brochure, please contact us at:
Ulverscroft Large Print Books Ltd.,
The Green, Bradgate Road, Anstey,
Leicester, LE7 7FU, England.
Tel: (00 44) **0116 236 4325**
Fax: (00 44) **0116 234 0205**

Other titles published by
The House of Ulverscroft:

WILD ABOUT HARRY

Roger Silverwood

Detective Inspector Angel and his team investigate a puzzling case of abduction and possible murder in the south Yorkshire town of Bromersley. A rich woman marries a man she hardly knows then disappears. Investigations reveal that her husband, Harry, never existed. Also, four men who claim they have nothing in common, staying at the Feathers Hotel, are attacked in their sleep, and each suffering from a painful broken finger. At the same time, a hit man, known as The Fixer, is at large, causing every villain and policeman to be apprehensive and on their toes . . .

BLEED A RIVER DEEP

Brian McGilloway

When a controversial US diplomat is attacked during the opening of Donegal gold mine, Inspector Benedict Devlin is disciplined for the lapse in security. The gunman turns out to be a young environmentalist named Leon Bradley — the brother of an old friend of Devlin's. The killing of an illegal immigrant near the Irish border leads Devlin to a vicious European people-smuggling ring. Then Bradley himself is found dead near the mine and Devlin begins to suspect that the business is a front for something far more sinister . . .

VENGEANCE DEFERRED

Peter Conway

Kate Farrant is chairperson of The Frampton Trust, a medical charity. During the night in the basement flat of her gambling club, Kate is overcome by a severe gastro-intestinal disorder and rings for an ambulance. When she later dies in hospital, it's discovered that she has been poisoned. Several people have reason to fear and hate her, and the investigation leads from the gambling club and those who'd worked at The Frampton Trust to the school where she and her psychopathic brother were pupils ten years earlier . . . Only then can any light be shed upon the identity of the murderer . . .

ON A THIN STALK

A. M. Story

At three in the morning by a disused airfield, jobbing farmer and local councillor Amos Cotswold leaps for his life when Spitfires strafe the road. He lands in a ditch atop the corpse of a German prisoner of war. But it's 2006. Could this be a ghostly repetition? Or powerful interests opposed to the redevelopment of the adjacent army camp? Amos comes up against phantom aircraft, fine art, and a gangmaster's exploitation of immigrant labour. Hampered by his inherited obligation to the wartime underground movement, Amos finally uncovers the dark reality of what the Second World War bequeathed the country.

1	21	41	61	81	101	121	141	161	181
2	22	42	62	82	102	122	142	162	182
3	23	43	63	83	103	123	143	163	183
4	24	44	64	84	104	124	144	164	184
5	25	45	65	85	105	125	145	165	185
6	26	46	66	86	106	126	146	166	186
7	27	47	67	87	107	127	147	167	187
8	28	48	68	88	108	128	148	168	188
9	29	49	69	89	109	129	149	169	189
10	30	50	70	90	110	130	150	170	190
11	31	51	71	91	111	131	151	171	191
12	32	52	72	92	112	132	152	172	192
13	33	53	73	93	113	133	153	173	193
14	34	54	74	94	114	134	154	174	194
15	35	55	75	95	115	135	155	175	195
16	36	56	76	96	116	136	156	176	196
17	37	57	77	97	117	137	157	177	197
18	38	58	78	98	118	138	158	178	198
19	39	59	79	99	119	139	159	179	199
20	40	60	80	100	120	140	160	180	200

201	216	231	246	261	276	291	306	321	336
202	217	232	247	262	277	292	307	322	337
203	218	233	248	263	278	293	308	323	338
204	219	234	249	264	279	294	309	324	339
205	220	235	250	265	280	295	310	325	340
206	221	236	251	266	281	296	311	326	341
207	222	237	252	267	282	297	312	327	342
208	223	238	253	268	283	298	313	328	343
209	224	239	254	269	284	299	314	329	344
210	225	240	255	270	285	300	315	330	345
211	226	241	256	271	286	301	316	331	346
212	227	242	257	272	287	302	317	332	347
213	228	243	258	273	288	303	318	333	348
214	229	244	259	274	289	304	319	334	349
215	230	245	260	275	290	305	320	335	350